The Adventures of
MENAHEM-MENDL

SHOLOM ALEICHEM

❦ ❦ ❦

The Adventures of
MENAHEM-MENDL

TRANSLATED FROM THE YIDDISH
BY TAMARA KAHANA

A PARAGON BOOK

Paragon Books
are published by
G. P. Putnam's Sons
200 Madison Avenue
New York, New York 10016

Library of Congress Cataloging in Publication Data

Rabinowitz, Shalom, 1859–1916.
    The adventures of Menahem-Mendl.

    (A Paragon book)
    Translation of Menahem-Mendl.
    I. Title.
PZ3.R113Ad   1979   [PJ5129.R2]   839'.09'33
79-13506
ISBN 0-399-50396-X

First Paragon Printing, 1979
Printed in the United States of America

FOREWORD

I ventured to translate Sholom Aleichem's *Menahem-Mendl*
for two reasons. The first is a personal one. This is one of my
favorite books—in any language—and for years I longed to see
it in an English translation in order to share my pleasure in it
with the reader of English. The second reason is my conviction
that while it is so rich and delightful for its idiom and style, it
is also memorable for its characterizations. I thought it a pity
that the English reader remain unacquainted with Menahem-
Mendl, that gentle, innocent lamb among the wolves, the
luftmensch who never ceases to build castles in the air, the
eternal ne'er-do-well and optimist with his unfailing confidence
in God, whose name is always on his lips; his scolding, queru-
lous, but ever-devoted and faithful wife, Sheineh-Sheindl, who
is always ready to lash him with her tongue and to succor him in
his most desperate moments; and his mother-in-law, whom we
know only through her pithy, vitriolic sayings. All three have
become part of the Jewish tradition. Every Yiddish-speaking
Jew knows a "Menahem-Mendl" in his neighbor (or perhaps in
himself), and some even think he was a real person. Well, perhaps he was—in the sense that Don Quixote was real.

Moreover, throughout this exchange of letters, we get a vivid
picture of Jewish life in the big cities and in the smaller towns
of Russia before the revolution. We learn how Jews lived in
Odessa and in Yehupetz (which is the city of Kiev in disguise),
in the Jewish summer resort of Boyarka (hiding under the name
of Boiberik), and—thanks to the letters of Sheineh-Sheindl—

in a typical small Jewish town like Kasrilevka (Sholom Aleichem's generic name for any poor people's town).

In this translation I was greatly aided by the guidance of my late father, I. D. Berkowitz, whose own masterly translations of Sholom Aleichem's books into Hebrew have become classic works.

TAMARA KAHANA

Tel Aviv

CONTENTS

INTRODUCTION

Sholom Aleichem started the letters of Menahem-Mendl in 1892. While getting them ready for publication in book form in 1909, he edited them himself, greatly shortening them and even rejecting a good many of them as unworthy of inclusion in a book.

These, therefore, are only part of the many Menahem-Mendl letters which were printed in various newspapers and periodicals over a period of eighteen years. Now that Sholom Aleichem's archives have found a permanent home in the Sholom Aleichem House in Tel Aviv, it is hoped that an academic edition of his works, including all works which have hitherto not appeared in book form, will be prepared.

Working on the principle that the average reader, like myself, dislikes footnotes and appendices in a work of fiction, I wish to make a number of explanatory comments which may help the reader understand certain aspects of Jewish-Russian life, which have been dimmed by distance and passage of time.

First, a few words about Menahem-Mendl's transactions on the stock exchanges of Odessa and Yehupetz. "London" must be understood as used in the sense of "sterling." The petty money speculators in Odessa were buying and selling Russian rubles (gold) against British pounds (sterling), making their profits out of rises ("hausses") or drops ("baisses") later in the day or, by the end of the day, in the value of the currency which they had sold. A "stallage" is an operation by which the speculator sells and buys the money of one country against the money of another country in the hope that by the time the sale or purchase is completed (whether at the end of the day or on any future specified date), the prices will rise or fall, so that he has a profit. A stallage, then, is actually a double operation, consisting of a buy *à la hausse* together with a sale *à la baisse* (from which Menahem-Mendl derives the corrupted terms "hausses" and "baisses"). For instance, if the speculator purchases rubles with pounds sterling in the hope that the price of the ruble will go up by the time of delivery, then he is buying *à la hausse;* at the same time (or a little later), fearing that he might have made a bad guess on the rise in the price of the ruble and that it might go down, he protects himself—that is, he hedges, by telling his broker to sell some rubles for him *à la baisse,* so that if indeed the rubles do go down in price by the time of the end of the deal, then he has cut his losses or even managed to make a small profit, depending on whether the two differences came out in his favor or against him. But the main thing to remember is that if the terms and operations seem confusing, *they certainly were confusing to Menahem-Mendl himself!*

The name of Brodsky occurs a number of times in the book. Lev Brodsky was a wealthy Russian-Jewish sugar manufacturer whose name, at the turn of the century, was as familiar to Russian Jews as the name of Rothschild to the world at large.

I shall not attempt to give a more accurate account of the notorious Dreyfus case in France than the one given by Menahem-Mendl, but anyone who desires to refresh his memory can turn to any reliable encyclopedia or volume of history.

A *heder* is a Hebrew school devoted solely to the study of the Bible and the Talmud.

Hassidism is a branch of Judaism, notable for its joyous approach to religion. A Hassid, then, is a follower of Hassidism.

In Yiddish, *Reb,* though stemming from "Rabbi," is simply an honorific, such as Mister, though it implies a degree of learning.

On the Jewish New Year there is a special grace for fruit which one had not eaten throughout the preceding year. In

Russia, this holiday coincided with the beginning of the grape season; therefore, on the New Year one pronounced grace over grapes—incidentally, a rare and expensive fruit in the north of Russia.

Eligibility for, and conscription into, the Russian army was a very sore point for Jews in Russia for reasons which will not be discussed here. The period of conscription was regularly four years, and there was practically no chance for Jews (who were, in any event, denied most civil rights) to receive promotion beyond the ranks. This is the reason why Sheineh-Sheindl thinks it incredible for the Jew Dreyfus to have been a captain in the army.

Purim, a spring holiday, is one of the gayest in the Jewish calendar; it commemorates the downfall of Haman (see the Book of Esther).

A *Litvak* is literally a Lithuanian, but for Jews it describes a certain type, rather dour, who had (perhaps undeservedly) a reputation for leaving his wife and going off to America.

In those days, marriages among Jews were mostly arranged through marriage brokers. When the parents of the prospective bride and groom (who were rarely consulted in the matter) reached an agreement in principle, a meeting would be arranged between the two parties to give them a chance to look each other over. The young people were also given an opportunity to meet, except in families of excessive orthodoxy, when bride and groom never set eyes on one another until the wedding day. The meeting was followed by the drawing up of a betrothal contract, ritually symbolized by breaking of dishes. This ceremony is the equivalent of the modern engagement.

In very pious families, right after the wedding, the bride had her hair cut off and thereafter wore a wig or otherwise kept her head covered. It was, in those days, a sign of great enlightenment or brazenness (depending on the point of view) to discard the wig.

In point of Jewish Law, for a marriage to be solemnized, it

is quite sufficient (though not usual) for a man to place a wedding ring on the forefinger of a young woman, in the presence of two male witnesses, and to pronounce a ritual phrase.

It was not the bride alone who brought a dowry. Often, in bourgeois circles, the groom's family was expected to contribute its share to set up the newlyweds. In cases of divorce, the divorcée would receive back what she had brought as her dowry.

It may perhaps be pointed out that ancestry to Jews was (and to a great degree still is) of no less importance than wealth, and perhaps even greater. A "good" family tree is one which can boast of learned men and famous rabbis, and this carried very great weight in arranging a marriage. The Jewish "aristocrat" is therefore not necessarily one who comes from a rich family, but one who has a long string of rabbis in his family tree.

The period of mourning is thirty days (*shloshim*—literally "thirty" in Hebrew) from the day of death. During the first seven days, the shivah (literally "seven" in Hebrew) is observed, when the mourners sit on the floor, shoeless, and eschew most of their usual activities. After the shivah, normal activities are permitted. Once the Thirty Days are over, the widows or widowers can remarry if they so choose.

In Czarist Russia, Jews were not allowed to live beyond the Pale—the Pale being the regions where Jews had permit of residence. There was a determined effort to keep them out of certain cities, especially in central Russia, such as Kiev and Moscow; Petersburg was also beyond the Pale. However, certain categories of Jews were given permits of residence in the forbidden cities. These were either professionals (lawyers, physicians, etc.) skilled workers, or merchants of the First Guild. Those Jews who penetrated such cities without benefit of permit led a hide-and-seek existence, as described in this book.

The beginning of each letter in the correspondence between Menahem-Mendl and his wife is a formal invocation, written in flowery Hebrew or a mixture of Hebrew and Yiddish, whereas the letters themselves were written in Yiddish.

A word about transliteration of names: On the whole, I tried to transcribe names phonetically. However, there were times when I felt that an exact phonetic transliteration would make for very difficult reading in English. For example, confronted with "Sooreh-Nechameh," I discarded it as too grotesque and substituted the more orthodox Hebrew pronunciation, "Sarah-Nehama," as easier on the eye.

T. K.

Book I
LONDON
The Stock Exchange in Odessa

I

Menahem-Mendl from Odessa to his wife,
Sheineh-Sheindl, in Kasrilevka

To my dear, wise, and modest helpmeet, Sheineh-Sheindl,
long may she live!

F i r s t l y, I am come to inform you that I am, by the
grace of God, well and in good cheer. May the Lord, blessed
be His name, grant that we always hear from one another
none but the best, the most comforting, and the happiest of
tidings—amen.

A n d S e c o n d l y, I want you to know that it is simply not in my power to describe the city of Odessa—how
big and how beautiful it is—the people here, so wonderful
and good-hearted, and the terrific business one can do here.

Just picture me with my cane walking along Greek Street
(that's the name of that Odessa Street where Jews are doing
business) and finding twenty thousand little deals awaiting
me: If it's wheat that I want, there is wheat for me; if it's
bran, there is bran here; if it's wool, that's here, too, as
well as flour and salt and feathers and raisins and sacks and
herrings—in short, anything the tongue can name may be
found in our Odessa City. At first I had my eye on a couple
of good little deals, but none was quite after my heart. So
I strolled along Greek Street until I finally hit on something really good. And so I am now dealing in London, and
I am not doing too badly at it. Once in a while you can pick
up twenty-five shekels; at other times, fifty; and if you're

really lucky, even a hundred. In short, London is the kind of business that can change your fortune overnight.

Not so long ago a character arrived here—a beadle or something—and before you could say, "Hear O Israel," he picked up thirty thousand. Today you can't get within a mile of him. I tell you, my dearest wife, gold is simply rolling in the streets; praise God, I do not in the least regret that I stopped off in Odessa. However, you're sure to ask how I managed to wind up in Odessa, considering that I was on my way to Kishinev. Well, it must have been written in the books that I am destined to make a fat pile! Wait and hear how the Almighty guides the steps of man.

When I arrived in Kishinev in order to retrieve from Uncle Menasheh the dowry money I had lent him, he asks me what do I need the dowry money for. So I tell him, I suppose I do need it; if I didn't, I wouldn't be here. Says he that he hasn't got a penny in cash at the moment, but he could, he says, give me a check on Brodsky in Yehupetz. Say I, very well, let it be Yehupetz, so long as there's money in it. Says he, he isn't really sure whether there is any money in Yehupetz at the moment. But he could, says he, give me a check on Bachrach in Warsaw. Say I, let it be Warsaw, so long as there's money in it. Says he, "What good is Warsaw to you? Warsaw is far away." If I want to, he says, he can give me a check on Barbash in Odessa. Say I, let it be Odessa, so long as there's money in it. So again he asks, "What do you need the money for?" And again I tell him that I suppose I do need it—if I didn't, I wouldn't be here.

To make a long story short, he squirms to the left, he squirms to the right, but it does him as much good as cupping to a corpse. Me—when I say money, I mean money! So he goes and makes out a couple of promissory notes, each one for five hundred rubles and good for only five months. He also gives me a check for three hundred rubles on Barbash in Odessa and the rest in cash—toward my expenses, he says. And since I am pressed for time, I must cut this short. In my next letter, please God, I'll write you everything in detail. Be well, greet the children, long may they live, and remember me kindly to your father and mother, to old and young, to big and small.

From me, your husband,
Menahem-Mendl.

Just remembered! When I came to Barbash with the check, I was told the check wasn't a check at all. So what is it? It's a glimpse into the distant future! First of all, they tell me, your Uncle Menasheh's wagonload of wheat has to arrive; after the wheat comes, it has to be sold for its full price; and only then can I get the money. Short and sweet! So I immediately sent a postcard to Kishinev and wrote him that if he doesn't send the wheat at once, I'll dash off a telegram to him. To make a long story short: a postcard here, a postcard there—I simply didn't know what to do for worry. And only yesterday did I receive from Kishinev one hundred in cash and two hundred in promissory notes. Do you understand now why I haven't written you all this time? I was certain that the three hundred rubles had gone down the drain. But this only shows that you mustn't always expect the worst. There is God in heaven who looks after you. I've put all the cash in London. I bought a whole pack of merchandise—hausses and baisses both—and, praise the Lord, I heard there's a profit already.

As above.

2

Sheineh-Sheindl from Kasrilevka to her husband, Menahem-Mendl, in Odessa

To my dear, esteemed, renowned, and honored husband, the wise and learned Menahem-Mendl, may his light shine forever.

In the first place, I want to let you know that we are all, praise the Lord, perfectly well, and may we hear the same from you, please God, and never anything worse.

In the second place, I am writing to say that I've had another attack of my old spasms which I'd be happy to hand over to your Uncle Menasheh who has made such a hash of the fifteen-hundred-ruble dowry, worse luck! As Mother says, God bless her, "It's like sending a cat to deliver the fish. . . ." Catch me taking promissory notes from him! May as well take the plague from him, a five-month fever! Look here, I wish I were telling a lie, but I'm afraid you have as much chance to set your eyes on the rest of that money as on the ears at the sides of your head which you've carried all the way to Odessa. Your luck that Mother doesn't know anything about those promissory notes, or you'd never hear the end of it. And as for the money which you write you are earning, praise the Lord, we are all happy to hear about it, Mendl. There is only one thing—may all my enemies enjoy eighty lean years —if you are already writing to me, why don't you write like a human being? Why don't you describe exactly what kind of merchandise you are handling? How much does it cost by the yard? Or maybe it is sold by weight? I still cannot make head or tail of it—how do you eat it, with a spoon or with a fork? And there's another thing I cannot understand: You say you bought merchandise, and it's already bringing in a profit. What kind of merchandise have you got hold of that rises like cake on yeast? "Even mushrooms," says Mother, God bless her, "need rain to make them grow. . . ." And if there is already a profit, why don't you sell? Are you waiting for a famine? And why don't you write where you are staying, and what are you feeding on? It's almost as if I were a stranger to you, not your wife till a hundred and twenty years, but some kind of concubine, perish the thought. As Mother says, God bless her, "When a cow leaves the herd, she forgets all her good intentions. . . ." If you listen to me, you'll sell your goods as quickly as possible. Better come and bring a bit of cash home, where you can find a finer business than the one you write about—I don't even know what it's called—I wish I knew as much about sorrow! So be well, which is the heartfelt wish of your really devoted wife,

Sheineh-Sheindl.

3

Menahem-Mendl from Odessa to his wife,
Sheineh-Sheindl, in Kasrilevka

To my dear, wise, and modest helpmeet, Sheineh-Sheindl,
long may she live!

Firstly, I am come to inform you that I am, by
the grace of God, well and in good cheer. May the Lord,
blessed be His name, grant that we always hear from one
another none but the best, the most comforting, and the
happiest of tidings—amen.

And Secondly, I want you to know that it does
not surprise me in the least that you cannot make head
or tail of London. Because if experienced merchants, Jews
with long beards, get snarled up in it, what can one expect
of a woman? I shall therefore try to make it clear to you so
that you'll understand exactly what it's all about. You see,
London is a very delicate kind of merchandise. It is sold
neither by the yard nor by weight, but on a word of honor.
What's more, you cannot see it with your eyes. It changes
every minute: Today it's expensive, tomorrow it's cheap;
today it's a hausse, tomorrow it's a baisse; today it's high,
tomorrow it's low. That is to say, over there in Berlin our
ruble either rises to the sky or else plunges to the ground.
It all depends on Berlin—whatever Berlin says goes. The
exchange keeps swinging up and down like mad; telegrams
fly back and forth, Jews scramble about like at a fair, buying and selling, rushing, pushing, shouting, making busi-

ness and getting rich—and me in the middle. There is such a noise and a tumult, it can shatter your eardrums. For example, only yesterday I made a little stallage which cost me a fifty, and today, exactly at noon, it evaporated like last winter's snow. But I don't suppose you even know what it means to make a stallage, so it must be explained to you. For example, you put up fifty for a day; the other fellow "sets the exchange," and you have the right to choose the kind of stallage you want—two hausses or two baisses. Or you can simply mark time, in which case the other fellow buys blind until the "close" (that's what we call twilight here in Odessa, which is just about the time that evening prayers are said in Kasrilevka). And if the exchange drops, you can kiss your fifty good-bye—and that's what is called making a stallage. But you are not to worry, my dearest wife! It's no great shakes to lose a fifty. The good Lord willing, everything will turn out for the best, and then, please God, the right moment will come, and I'll make money, and maybe even a lot of it!

And as for what you say about Uncle Menasheh's promissory notes, you are making a big mistake. Uncle Menasheh's sun has not gone down yet, and he is still a good risk. If I wanted to make a small reduction, I could find plenty of customers. But I don't want to. If I need any cash, I can get plenty. All I have to do is sell a couple of hausses or a couple of baisses. But I don't feel like doing that either. I'll do better by buying another stallage. The more stallages, the better. When you go to bed with a stallage, you sleep all the sweeter. And since I am pressed for time, I must cut this short. Please God, in my next letter I'll write you everything in detail. For the time being, may the Lord grant health and success,

From me, your husband,
Menahem-Mendl.

Just remembered! You ask where I'm staying and what I'm eating. To tell you the truth, my dearest wife, I myself don't know where I am. The city of Odessa is terribly big, everything is expensive, and here the houses are as tall as the sky—you have to climb an iron staircase for half an hour before you reach your lodging, which is right under the clouds, and the window is a tiny one, like in jail. I'm happy to see daybreak when I can escape from this jail into Greek Street, and that's where I always eat, standing up. That is to say, you grab whatever comes your way, because who's got the time to sit down properly to eat when you have constantly to watch the Berlin exchange? However, fruit is very cheap here. You don't eat grapes here like in Kasrilevka, where you eat them only on New Year's when you say grace; here everybody eats grapes every single day, right in the middle of the street, and nobody is ashamed of it.

As above.

4

Sheineh-Sheindl from Kasrilevka to her husband, Menahem-Mendl, in Odessa

To my dear, esteemed, renowned, and honored husband, the wise and learned Menahem-Mendl, may his light shine forever.

In the first place, I want to let you know that we are all, praise the Lord, perfectly well, and may we hear the same from you, please God, and never anything worse.

In the second place, I am writing to say that I believe you must have gone out of your mind. May I be spared ever seeing head or tail of your wonderful Odessa, if I can make head or tail of all your chatter about stallages and baggages, hausses and baisses and all other messes, the devil knows what they are! And fifties are flying out of your hands like hot doughnuts. Money seems to mean nothing to you; it's just dirt! I'm sure anybody can bathe in gold if they engage in such business deals! Even if you were to chop my head off, I still wouldn't understand what kind of merchandise it can be if it's invisible. A cat in a sack? . . . Listen to me, Mendl, I don't like it. In my father's home, I wasn't accustomed to such airy affairs, and may the Almighty continue to preserve me from them. As Mother says, God bless her, "From the air, all one can catch is a cold. . . ." You write: "When you go to bed with a baggage, you sleep all the sweeter. . . ." Whoever goes

to bed with a baggage? What strange expressions you use—
they sound Turkish to me! And as for what you say about
cashing in Uncle Menasheh's notes, if I refuse to believe
you, nobody will consider me an infidel. As Mother says,
God bless her, "Until you count your pennies twice, you
can never be sure. . . ." You know something, Mendl?
Listen to me, to your wife—finish off with this Odessa of
yours, and come home to Kasrilevka! Have you got fifteen
hundred in your pocket? Does Father, God bless him, give
us a place to live in? Are there shops for rent? So what else
do you want! Why must I be on the tip of everyone's tongue
and have my enemies whisper that you've run away from
me to Odessa and abandoned me, may you never live to see
that day! In the meantime, your Odessa can answer for the
sins of our Kasrilevka, with all your tall houses and iron
stairs that have to be climbed like mad! Is it worth it, to
spoil your stomach for Odessa's sake? What's all the excitement about! Because grapes are terribly cheap? Do you have
to gorge on grapes—are plums poison? This year we have
plenty of plums, a penny a bucket! But you don't seem to
care very much about what goes on at home. You don't
even ask what the children are doing. It looks as if you've
quite forgotten that you are father to three little ones, God
bless them. As Mother says, "Out of sight, out of mind.
. . ." You can burst if you will, but she is always right.
Meanwhile, be well, and the best of luck to you, which is
the heartfelt wish of your really devoted wife,

Sheineh-Sheindl.

5

Menahem-Mendl from Odessa to his wife,
Sheineh-Sheindl, in Kasrilevka

To my dear, wise, and modest helpmeet, Sheineh-Sheindl,
long may she live!

F i r s t l y, I am come to inform you that I am, by the
grace of God, well and in good cheer. May the Lord, blessed
be His name, grant that we always hear from one another
none but the best, the most comforting, and the happiest
of tidings—amen.

A n d S e c o n d l y, I want you to know that just now
there is a terrific upswing of baisses, I have therefore
stuffed myself up with London, and I've made a stock of
seventeen baisses and eight stallages. Besides, since I'm
to get several hundred rubles in differences, I'll be able to
make some more baisses, please God. If, my dearest wife,
you could only see how business is conducted here on a
word of honor, you'd immediately understand what is
Odessa; a nod of the head is as good as a signature to a contract. I go for a stroll along Greek Street, walk into a "café,"
sit down at a small table and order a glass of tea or coffee
or something. Up comes one broker, then another, and then
a third. There's no need of a contract or a receipt, not even
pen and ink! Every broker carries a little notebook and a
pencil. He takes out his notebook and writes that I'm down
for two baisses with him, and all I have to do is pay him
several shekels. It's a pleasure! And a few hours later when,

God willing, the news arrives from Berlin about the rate of exchange, that very same broker comes running and gives you a twenty-five. A little later, when you already know the opening price, he forces a fifty on you, and still later, at the close, it grows to a hundred, please God. And sometimes it can be two hundred, and even three hundred—why not? That's the stock exchange for you! The stock exchange is a game of chance, a matter of luck.

And as for what you write about not believing in Uncle Menasheh's promissory notes, I have news for you: I've already found customers for them. If you want proof, here it is: Where else did I get the money for so many baisses and stallages? By the way, it is stallage and not baggage as you call it. And since you ask how one can go to bed with a stallage, I can see that you still don't understand what it's all about. A stallage is a piece of paper on which the other fellow writes that when the "ultimo" (that is, the end of the month) comes, he is obliged to give to you—or perhaps, the other way around, to take from you—a certain number of pounds according to a certain exchange. That is to say, the choice is up to you: If you feel like it, you pay; if you don't feel like it, you receive. Now do you understand the science of stallages? If, please God, there are strong "variations" in London, and for example, the newspapers start talking about war, then the Russian ruble takes a flying dive into the depths of the earth, and London gives a leap till you can't see it above the clouds. Only last week they were saying about the English Queen that she wasn't in the best of health. Immediately the Russian ruble dropped, and stallages jumped to the roof. Now the newspapers are saying she is feeling better, so the Russian ruble is up again, and today you can get as many stallages as you want. In short, you are not to worry, my dearest wife, for, God willing, as we say in Odessa, "Everything is going to be Class A"! And since I am pressed for time, I must cut this short. Please God, in my next letter I'll write you everything in detail. For the time being, may the Lord grant health and success. Please greet the children, God bless them, and give my kindest regards to everyone, to old and young, to big and small.

From me, your husband,
Menahem-Mendl.

Just remembered! It is so hot in our Odessa, that during the day you sizzle, and at night you melt like wax. Therefore, as soon as it gets dark, the city empties completely. Everybody goes away to the springs—either the Big Spring or the Little Spring. There you can have everything your heart desires: You can bathe in the sea, and you can listen to music free of charge, without paying a penny!

As above.

6

Sheineh-Sheindl from Kasrilevka to her husband, Menahem-Mendl, in Odessa

To my dear, esteemed, renowned, and honored husband, the wise and learned Menahem-Mendl, may his light shine forever.

In the first place, I want to let you know that we are all, praise the Lord, perfectly well, and may we hear the same from you, please God, and never anything worse.

In the second place, I am writing to say that I am again having trouble with my teeth, may all your wonderful Odessa music makers, big and little, enjoy such a pain! I have to suffer here from toothache and worry myself sick over his children, and he—nothing at all! He is living happily ever after in Odessa; he is riding around on springs, bathing in big and little fountains, while musicians play for him! What else does he want! As Mother says, God bless her, "I'd have him ride on a broom, not on springs. . . ." Make up your mind! If you are a merchant and if you are dealing in that wonderful merchandise called London, then attend to your business, and not to the English Queen! Better think of your wife—you've got a wife till a hundred and twenty years, and three little children, God bless them. As Mother says, "Think of your own and yourself—leave the rest on the shelf. . . ." And as for all those successes you write me about, I must confess they make my head spin. Somehow, kill me, but I still can't believe that hundreds of rubles are popping straight into your pockets. Is it some magic over there or sorcery, or a spell, or something? Better take care that with all your triumphs you do not touch a penny of the dowry money, because if you should, you won't hear the last of it from Mother, God bless her! You'd think he could give a thought to what's needed at home, at least. You know well enough that I can't possibly do without a silk coat and some serge for a dress and two pieces of linen cloth. I have to remind him of every little thing—the poor wretch has lost his memory; you'd think his brains have dried out! As Mother says, God bless her, "If a dig in the ribs doesn't work, try a brick. . . ." Which is the heartfelt wish of your really devoted wife,

Sheineh-Sheindl.

7

*Menahem-Mendl from Odessa to his wife,
Sheineh-Sheindl, in Kasrilevka*

To my dear, wise, and modest helpmeet, Sheineh-Sheindl,
long may she live!

F i r s t l y, I am come to inform you that I am, by the
grace of God, well and in good cheer. May the Lord,
blessed be His name, grant that we always hear from one
another none but the best, the most comforting and the
happiest of tidings—amen.

A n d S e c o n d l y, I want you to know that I've
made very good headway. That is to say, I'm up to my neck
in baisses, and I am now very busy with London. This means
that in one shot I hand out, or receive, as much as ten thousand pounds, twenty thousand pounds—on an "option," of
course. Already I have access to all the business offices and
am even privileged to sit in Café Fanconi, side by side with
all the big speculators at the white marble tables, and order a portion of ice cream, because in our Odessa it is the
custom that as soon as you sit down, up comes a man
dressed in a coat with a tail and orders you to order ice
cream. And since you cannot be an exception, you have to
order it. And when you finish your portion of ice cream, he
orders you to order another portion—if you don't, you're
not allowed to remain. Then you have to loiter in the
streets, which isn't quite nice for a speculator, and besides,
there's a policeman in the street who looks for loiterers.

. . . However, since Jews do have to loiter, we try to evade him. We play hide-and-seek with him and generally manage to fool him. But if he succeeds in catching anyone, he pounces on his precious prey and takes the treasure straight to the police station, as one might say, "Look, I've brought you a Jew. . . ."

And as for your saying that you don't believe in my "variations" and "differences," it only goes to show that you're weak in politics. For instance, in our Café Fanconi, there is a man we call Gambetta. Day in, day out, he talks politics and nothing but politics! In a thousand ways he can prove to you that there's a smell of war in the air. He says that every single night he can hear cannon shots—not here, but over there, in France. The French, he says, will never forget that man Bismarck as long as they live. He says, war simply must break out soon—it can't be otherwise. If you listen to Gambetta preach, you feel you have to sell everything you own, down to your coat, in order to buy up stallages and baisses, baisses without end!

And as for what you write about me buying you a coat, well, my dearest wife, I've got an eye on something much better for you—namely, a golden watch with a medallion, a golden chain, and a brooch, and I also saw some bracelets in one shopwindow, as a matter of fact, not far from Fanconi's, and I tell you, they're Class A! And since I am pressed for time, I must cut this short. Please God, in my next letter I'll write you everything in detail. For the time being, may the Lord grant health and success.

From me, your husband,
Menahem-Mendl.

Just remembered! There is such prosperity here, knock on wood, and people are so busy doing business that one loses sight of Sabbaths and holidays. For me, of course, Sabbath always is Sabbath. It can rain stones from the sky, but on Sabbath I've got to drop into the synagogue. The Odessa synagogue is something to see. First of all, it is called the Choir Synagogue because on top of it there's a round cap instead of a roof, and it hasn't got an East Wall. That is to say, everybody sits facing the cantor. And as for the cantor (Pinney is his name, and what a voice!), it's true he doesn't wear a beard, but he cannot be compared to that old drone of yours, Cantor Moishe Dovid! You ought to hear him pray—it can drive you out of your wits! As for his Sabbath day psalm, it is worthwhile buying a ticket to hear it. All the little choirboys stand around him in their little prayer shawls—what a pleasure! If Sabbath were to fall twice a week, I'd go twice a week to listen to Pinney. I cannot understand the Jews of Odessa— why don't they go to the synagogue to pray? And even those who do go to pray don't pray; they sit like puppets with their fat and shiny faces; they wear top hats on their heads; their prayer shawls are small and skimpy, and— shsh!—nobody even opens his mouth. And if some Jew should venture to pray a little louder, up comes the beadle with shiny buttons and says, "Quiet, please!" Funny Jews in Odessa!

As above.

8

Sheineh-Sheindl from Kasrilevka to her husband, Menahem-Mendl, in Odessa

To my dear, esteemed, renowned, and honored husband, the wise and learned Menahem-Mendl, may his light shine forever.

I n t h e f i r s t p l a c e, I want to let you know that we are all, praise the Lord, perfectly well, and may we hear the same from you, please God, and never anything worse.

I n t h e s e c o n d p l a c e, I am writing to say, my dearest husband, that I cannot understand what's so wonderful about having to sit at marble tables in Franconi's, may she burn to an ash, and gorge on what-do-you-call-it from morning till night. Just to throw money away? And who is that madman who wanders around your Odessa dreaming about cannon shots—may he get shot full of holes himself! Wars—is that what he hankers after? As Mother says, God bless her, "What's blood to you is water to him. . . ." Oh, so you've seen golden watches and bracelets in Odessa shopwindows! You can save them for your grandmother! What earthly use to me are presents which you see through windowpanes, Mendl? As Mother says, God bless her, "Pancakes seen in a dream aren't pancakes, only a dream. . . ." Better walk straight into a shop and buy me some linen for bedsheets and pillowcases, and a couple of woolen blankets, and some table silver for the

house, and whatnot. Just imagine, Blumeh-Zlateh finds it
necessary to stick her nose up at me. Her head is swollen
twice its size with pride, may she swell till she bursts! And
for why? Because she is wearing a string of pearls around
her neck, may it choke her! Well, she has it sweet with her
husband! Some people have all the luck; it's only me who
was born in such a dark and miserable hour that I've got to
remind him of every little thing! Try to imagine that you
are spending your money on another baisse, another
mess, and all those other things which only the devil knows
what they are and which I cannot even pronounce. I
keep telling him: Sell whatever you have and count your
change—so he goes and buys more! What are you afraid
of? That you won't get any of this merchandise later on?
I can see it all very plain now—what kind of business
you're doing and what kind of town Odessa is, where a Sabbath is not a Sabbath, and a holiday is not a holiday, and
where the cantor struts around with a shaved chin, may
all my sins fall on his head! To my mind, from such people
and from such a town one ought to run away like from a
putrid swamp. But there he is, wallowing in it without
any intention of budging. As Mother says, God bless her,
"The worm inside the radish thinks there's no sweeter
place. . . ." And so, my dearest husband, I am writing you
to think over carefully what you are doing and to stop frisk-
ing around your sweet Odessa, may it burn to an ash,
which is the heartfelt wish of your really devoted wife,

Sheineh-Sheindl.

Oh, yes! Please tell me, Mendl, who is Franconi, with
whom you seem to be spending all your days and nights?
Is it a he or a she? . . .

9

Menahem-Mendl from Odessa to his wife,
Sheineh-Sheindl, in Kasrilevka

To my dear, wise, and modest helpmeet, Sheineh-Sheindl,
long may she live!

F i r s t l y , I am come to inform you that I am, by the
grace of God, well and in good cheer. May the Lord, blessed
be His name, grant that we always hear from one another
none but the best, the most comforting, and the happiest
of tidings—amen.

A n d S e c o n d l y , I want you to know that already
there is a smell of heavy money in the air! If the ultimo
passes without a hitch, I'll be on the top rung, God willing. Then I'll cash in all my "differences," start out for
home and, please God, take you to Odessa with me. We'll
rent an apartment on Richelieu Street, buy some nice
furniture, and start the kind of life one can have only in
our Odessa. In the meantime, I'm having a little trouble
with my stomach, may you be spared the same. It looks as
if all that ice cream has upset it. . . . Now, when I come
to Fanconi's, I don't eat ice cream anymore. So what do I
do? I order a drink which you sip through a straw; it's
sweet and a little bitter all in one, it tastes like salty
licorice, and you can't possibly manage more than two or,
at the most, three glasses of it at a sitting. So the rest of
the time you have to go loiter outside and have dealings
with the policeman, which isn't at all pleasant. He's had

an eye on me for some days, but the Lord has been good, and I've managed to evade him every time and to hide from him. What doesn't a Jew do for a living? If, with the help of heaven, the "settlement" goes without a hitch, I'll buy you double of everything you want, please God, more than you ever dreamed of.

And when you say that Gambetta is a madman, you are making a mistake; he is simply rather quick-tempered. Heaven preserve anyone from saying something about politics that he doesn't fancy! Then he is capable of tearing you limb from limb. He claims that something is liable to explode any day now, and, he says, the mere fact that at the moment everything is suddenly quiet certainly points to war. "There is always," he says, "a lull before a storm. . . ." Yesterday I had a chance to sell several baisses, as well as two or three stallages, and to make a good profit, but Gambetta wouldn't let me do it. He said, "I'll break your head if at a time like this you will let the tiniest bit of merchandise slip out of your fingers!" The hour is close, he says, when a fifty-ruble stallage will be worth two hundred, three hundred, five hundred, a thousand—and why not even two thousand? . . . If it is as Gambetta says—or even half of what he says—I'm bound to get rich! Right after the settlement, I hope, please God, to switch back to hausses, start buying up rubles, and give London a fine runaround. I'll show them the difference between London and a ruble! And since I am pressed for time, I must cut this short. Please God, in my next letter I'll write you everything in detail. For the time being, may the Lord grant health and success.

From me, your husband,
Menahem-Mendl.

Just remembered! As for what you ask about Fanconi (not "Franconi" as you say), it's neither a he nor a she. It is simply a coffeehouse where you drink coffee, eat ice cream, and deal in London. I wish I had at least half the money that changes hands there in a single day!

As above.

IO

Sheineh-Sheindl from Kasrilevka to her husband, Menahem-Mendl, in Odessa

To my dear, esteemed, renowned, and honored husband, the wise and learned Menahem-Mendl, may his light shine forever.

In the first place, I want to let you know that we are all, praise the Lord, perfectly well, and may we hear the same from you, please God, and never anything worse.

In the second place, I am writing to say that the children are down with the measles, all three of them, and I don't sleep nights, while he is sitting there drinking vinegar with licorice! Has he anything in his head to worry about—a headache maybe? And just listen to all the excitement—he's going to take me to Odessa! He thinks all he has to do is say, "Odessa," and I'll fly there like a shot. Listen, Mendl, get that silly idea out of your head; Mendl, you won't talk me into going there; Mendl, you can be sure of that! My great-grandmother was never there and managed to get along without it, so I suppose I, too, can manage without Odessa. You're not going to persuade me, Mendl, to leave my father and mother and all my good friends and go to your cursed Odessa, may it burn to an ash! You can say what you will, Mendl, but your Odessa is beginning to get under my skin. I don't know why, but I hate it. My good sense tells me you ought to sell your merchandise gradually and turn it into money. As Mother

says, God bless her, "The best of all dairy dishes is—a piece
of meat. . . ." So what? Are you afraid to let a bargain slip
through your fingers? Let the others enjoy it! And as
for your madman Gambet who doesn't allow you to sell
(I tell you again, he's a madman!), I don't understand what
he has to do with it! What concern are your grandmother's
worries to him? Send him to the blazes together with all
his war stories! Listen to me, Mendl: Cash in your affairs,
and sell everything while the good Lord is still watching
over you. Did you manage to earn a little money? Enough!
How long are you going to waste away there? But what's
the use—do I carry any weight with you? After all I'm only
Sheineh-Sheindl and not Blumeh-Zlateh. When Blumeh-
Zlateh utters one twitter, it throws her husband into a nine-
year fever! For heaven's sake, Mendl my dear, sell everything, pack up and come home! Only don't forget to buy a
dozen embroidered shifts for me, some velvet material for
a frock for Mother (let her remember that her son-in-law
was once in Odessa and did business with madmen)—also a
length of fashionable printed cotton and, if you can manage
to squeeze them into your suitcase, some glassware and any
other things you may think useful, and come home, so
the whole world should stop pointing their fingers at me
and jeering at me. Well, we'll see whether you'll listen to
me! May my enemies live to see the day you take my advice, which is the heartfelt wish of your really devoted wife,

Sheineh-Sheindl.

II

*Menahem-Mendl from Odessa to his wife,
Sheineh-Sheindl, in Kasrilevka*

To my dear, wise, and modest helpmeet, Sheineh-Sheindl,
long may she live!

Firstly, I am come to inform you that I am, by the
grace of God, well and in good cheer. May the Lord, blessed
be His name, grant that we always hear from one another
none but the best, the most comforting, and the happiest
of tidings—amen.

And Secondly, I want you to know that the ultimo arrived and turned everything upside down, may
heaven preserve us. The great variations, which I awaited
like the Messiah's coming, went up in smoke. Bismarck,
they say, caught a cold, so a terrible panic started up in
politics, and nobody knows what's what. London is now
actually worth its weight in gold, and our ruble has actually dropped down into the deepest cellar, and a terrible
baisse has set in! So you're sure to ask what happened to
all my baisses and my stallages? The answer is that baisses aren't baisses, and stallages aren't stallages—nobody
wants to take; nobody wants to give—and what are you
going to do about it? As in spite, I got my affairs entangled
with little people who were choked by the first squeeze. In
a word, this is an earthquake, a disaster, a catastrophe—you
wouldn't recognize the place! Oh, had I made an about-

face in time! But who can be a prophet? All the people are scurrying round like poisoned rats. There's a panic everywhere. Everyone is yelling, London! Where is my London? Give me London, London! But where is London? What is London? Slaps are flying, blows, insults, curses—and me in the middle. The point is there is no London and there never was!

In short, my dearest wife, everything looks dark and bitter. I've lost everything I made—profits, my capital, and the jewelry I bought you; I even had to strip off my Sabbath coat and pawn it—everything has gone down the drain. . . . You can't imagine the state I'm in, and I'm so homesick I am wasting away! A hundred times a day I curse the day I was born. Better to have broken both my legs before I ever came to Odessa, where a man counts for nothing. You can drop dead walking in the middle of the street, and nobody will even stop to look. How many brokers made a living around me and enjoyed plenty of tidbits on my account! And today not one of them even recognizes me! Before, I had a name here—they called me the Rothschild of Kasrilevka—and today they are making fun of me—those very same brokers! To hear them talk, I don't understand a thing about this business. "London," they say, "is an art that has to be understood." Where were they before, those sages? Things have come to such a pass that nobody talks about me anymore—I might as well be dead! And I wish I were dead rather than face such disgrace. And for spite, that cursed Gambetta sits there and doesn't stop dinning politics in my ear. "Ah," he says, "didn't I keep saying baisses?" "What good," say I, "are your baisses when nobody gives me London!" He laughs and says, "Whose fault is it? One has to understand the stock exchange. And if one doesn't know how to deal in London," he says, "one should stick to rags and old bottles. . . ." I tell you, my dearest wife, I am so sick of Odessa, its stock exchange, its Fanconi, and all those petty people, I'd be glad to run away anywhere! And since I am pressed for time, I must cut this short. Please God, in my next letter I'll write you everything in detail. For the time being, may the Lord grant health and success. Greet all the children, God bless them, and give my kindest regards to your father and mother, to old and young, to big and small.

From me, your husband,
Menahem-Mendl.

J u s t r e m e m b e r e d! There is a peculiar custom in this Odessa City—whenever anybody needs help, he doesn't go to a neighbor, a relative, or a friend, as we do in Kasrilevka, for example. Not because it's shameful, but simply because you know beforehand that you won't get even a fig, and that's all there is to it. So what does one do in time of need? They fixed up a place called pawnshop which gives you as much money as you want, so long as you bring them good security—it may be gold; it may be silver; it may be copper, or a suit, or a samovar, or a chair—even if you bring a cow, you can raise money on it! The only snag is that they put a very low value on anything you bring—less than nothing. On the other hand, there is one advantage: The interest they take is so nice and fat that it eats up your capital. So every two weeks they hold an "auction." That means, they sell all the securities which have not been redeemed, and people can get wonderful bargains and make a pretty penny on them. If I could lay my hand on some money now, I'd take a stab at doing business with a pawnshop, maybe get back what I lost, and perhaps even make a bit extra. . . . But what's the use? Without money, one should not be born into this world, and if one does get born, it is better to die. . . . I cannot write anymore. Let me know how you are feeling and what the children are doing, God bless them, and give my kindest greetings to your father and mother.

As above.

12

*Sheineh-Sheindl from Kasrilevka to her
husband, Menahem-Mendl, in Odessa*

To my dear, esteemed, renowned, and honored husband,
the wise and learned Menahem-Mendl, may his light shine
forever.

In the first place, I want to let you know that
we are all, praise the Lord, perfectly well, and may we hear
the same from you, please God, and never anything worse.

In the second place, I am writing to say, you
foolish simpleton, just look and see what you've done!
What ill wind has driven you to Odessa? What was it that
smelled so good to you there? Roast pigeons—is that what
you were longing for? London! Ice cream! Vinegar and
licorice! The moment you saw yourself getting stuck with
London, why didn't you settle on a percentage in time
and save at least part of your goods, you donkey? The way
merchants do! And why don't you appeal to arbitrators, to
a rabbi? God in heaven—ultimo—what has that got to
do with business? You bought merchandise, didn't you?
Well, what happened to the merchandise—where did it
go? What a calamity! But didn't I feel it in my bones that
nothing good would come of Odessa, may it burn to an
ash? I keep writing to him: Leave that town, Mendl, send
it to blazes together with London, and may a plague sweep
over it! I say to him: Run, Mendl, run! As Mother says,

"The higher the fool, the greater the fall. . . ." But no, he won't listen to me, because who am I? I am Sheineh-Sheindl, worse luck! I am not Blumeh-Zlateh. Oh, my mother is really wise! How many times did she say that a clever woman mustn't give her husband too much rope, that a wife must keep such a firm hold on her husband that never for a moment does he forget he's got a wife! But what am I to do if it isn't my nature? I wasn't born coarse like Blumeh-Zlateh. I can't nag or scold or shout or curse like she! If you had Blumeh-Zlateh for a wife, may she never live to see the day, you'd find out quick enough what the Almighty can do!

And as for what you say about dying, you sage, it only shows what a dolt you are. Man doesn't live by his own will, nor does he die by his own will. What if one does lose a whole dowry—is that sufficient reason for a hasty act? You simpleton, where is it written that Menahem-Mendl has to get rich? Isn't Menahem-Mendl with money the same as Menahem-Mendl without money? Fool, can one defy God? Don't you see, He was against it? So stop squirming! Let the money be your scapegoat forever! Just imagine that robbers attacked you in the middle of a forest, or what if you fell sick, God forbid, and the dowry went to the devil on medicines? The main thing—don't behave like a woman, Mendl! Put your trust in the Eternal One. He is your staff and your sustenance. Come home and, please God, you'll be a welcome guest among your children. . . .

I am sending you some money for traveling expenses, but see to it, Mendl, that you don't get involved in any deals, and don't buy rags and old bottles—that would be the last straw! As soon as you receive this letter with the money, for heaven's sake, hurry up and say good-bye forever to your Odessa, and the moment you leave that town, may it catch fire at all four ends, and may the fire burn and smoulder and splutter and crackle and rage till not a single stick or stone is left, not even an ash, which is the heartfelt wish of your really devoted wife,

Sheineh-Sheindl.

Book II
PAPERS
The Yehupetz Stock Exchange

I

Menahem-Mendl from Yehupetz to his wife,
Sheineh-Sheindl, in Kasrilevka

To my dear, wise, and modest helpmeet, Sheineh-Sheindl,
long may she live!

F i r s t l y, I am come to inform you that I am, by the
grace of God, well and in good cheer. May the Lord,
blessed be His name, grant that we always hear from one
another none but the best, the most comforting, and the
happiest of tidings—amen.

A n d S e c o n d l y, I want you to know that I am no
longer in Odessa. I am now in Yehupetz, also a fine, beautiful city—may my luck be as fine! And I am no longer
dealing in wind, in air, or in London—I now have my
hand, praise the Lord, on a more decent business, a more
solid business—a paper business. That is to say, I am dealing in papers. You'll probably ask how I got to Yehupetz.
Well, I have a whole story to tell you, my dearest wife, and
I must beg you to forgive me for not having written you
for such a long time. I simply did not have anything to
write about. Besides, I was on the verge of returning home
any day. God is my witness that I longed to be back home,
but it was evidently in the books that I should blunder
into Yehupetz and start dealing in papers. I swear, my
dearest wife, that I was already in the train on my way to
Kasrilevka when I had to run into an Odessa speculator
who was going to Yehupetz. What, I ask him, is his busi-

ness in Yehupetz? Says he to me, he deals in papers. What does that mean—papers? So he explains that papers are not at all like London, which depends on Berlin, Bismarck, and the English Queen. Papers is a kind of business which depends only on Petersburg and on Warsaw. Besides, it has another advantage: Papers are something you can actually see, touch and handle—not like London which is a thing of the imagination, a kind of dream. Then he began to praise to the skies the city of Yehupetz and the Yehupetz speculators: Everything is quite different there. The people are fine, pleasant, and honest. He would not, he says, give ten fat Odessa citizens for one Yehupetz speculator. In short, the fellow got me so interested that I felt I simply had to see that city for myself. Since I was passing the station of Fastov anyway, I could just as well drop into Yehupetz to satisfy my curiosity and take a look at their stock exchange and their speculators.

Well, it was evidently God's will that I should arrive just when the papers were falling headlong and premiums were being sold at half price. As there was no need to invest a lot of cash, I decided to try it out—maybe I'll be lucky this time, pick something up, and make enough to cover the expenses of the detour. And the good Lord evidently took pity on me: The papers leaped; I sold my premiums with a profit and bought a number of fresh premiums. And again I was lucky and wound up with a fine bunch of hundreds—in cash, too. So I thought the matter over: Why should I pay premiums to other people? Why shouldn't I acquire some papers of my own? So I immediately got hold of Petersburg by way of an agency and assembled a portfolio of all kinds of gems: Putilov, Transport, Volga, Maltzev—and similar shares which are on their way up. And thank God, I am growing! And since I am pressed for time, I must cut this short. Please God, in my next letter

I'll write you everything in detail. For the time being, may the Lord grant health and success. Greet the children, God bless them, and give my kindest regards to your mother and father, to old and young, to big and small.

From me, your husband,
Menahem-Mendl.

J u s t   r e m e m b e r e d! When you write me, please address your letters to Boiberik because I'm not allowed to stay in Yehupetz. . . . All day long I traipse along the street called Kreshchatik and around the exchange, and when night falls, I hurry off to Boiberik. There in the summer cottages, a whole crowd of speculators spend their time playing cards all night long (males and females together—that's the custom here). And early in the morning everybody rushes off to Yehupetz, and me in the middle.

As above.

2

Sheineh-Sheindl from Kasrilevka to her husband, Menahem-Mendl, in Yehupetz

To my dear, esteemed, renowned, and honored husband, the wise and learned Menahem-Mendl, may his light shine forever.

In the first place, I want to let you know that we are all, praise the Lord, perfectly well, and may we hear the same from you, please God, and never anything worse.

In the second place, I am writing to say, my dearest husband, that I wish my enemies had as much strength to keep alive as I have to write even these few words to you, for I can hardly drag my feet. It is quite possible that I'll have to have a reparation—that's what the new doctor proposes—may heaven propose to send him all the seven plagues! He thinks I'm a bottomless money box where he can fish for rubles without end! And what do you think is the cause of it all? Nothing but aggravation, nothing but heartache. This is unheard of—I send you money for traveling expenses and tell you to come straight home, and you take this money and go straight to Yehupetz! Shouldn't you be buried alive for it? And the shame of it! I cannot look anyone in the eyes! As Mother says, God bless her, "If your nose is running, don't face the wind. . . ." Business! Deals! I thought it was all done and finished with your wonderful "London." I thought the good Lord might take pity on me and he'll come home at least with his life intact, my dearest breadwinner. And what's the result? A new dream—a nightmare—Yehupetz! Papers! What a business! Who ever heard of a Jew dealing in scraps of paper? . . . I have read your letter, my dearest husband, and I keep saying to myself: God in heaven, merciful Father! Is it you who is mad, perish the thought, or is it I who am not quite right in the head? You sound as if you're talking Greek: "Papers," "Petersburg," "Kreshchatik," "Potfolio." . . . An evil spirit must have entered him. By day he's in Yehupetz, and at night he's in Boiberik with men and women together. . . . What are you doing in Boiberik at night? What can you be thinking of? Make up your mind: Don't you want me? So come home and give me a divorce. Otherwise, you may as well go with all the four winds to America like Yossl, Arieh-Leib's son-in-law, so I shouldn't know where your bones are moldering, if I am destined forever to remain an abandoned wife with little fledgling children! But my enemies won't live to see that day! It is your undeserved luck that I am now in no condition to travel. The Lord has punished me, and I am bedridden. As Mother says, God bless her, "If you haven't any fingers, you can't thumb your nose. . . ." Otherwise, right after receiving your wonderful letter, I would have gone straight to you and brought you home already. I'd show you what a wife is! What if I do let a harsh word slip out once in a while? That happens only from aggravation, and it never lasts long. As Mother says, God bless her, "A match is quick to splutter and quick to go out. . . ." Which is the heartfelt wish of your really devoted wife,

　　　　　　　　　Sheineh-Sheindl.

3

Menahem-Mendl from Yehupetz to his wife,
Sheineh-Sheindl, in Kasrilevka

To my dear, wise, and modest helpmeet, Sheineh-Sheindl,
long may she live!

F i r s t l y, I am come to inform you that I am, by the
grace of God, well and in good cheer. May the Lord,
blessed be His name, grant that we always hear from one
another none but the best, the most comforting, and the
happiest of tidings—amen.

A n d   S e c o n d l y, I want you to know that the paper
business is not—as you seem to think—really paper. It is
only called papers—actually they are shares: Petersburg
shares. For example, Putilov, Transport, Volga, Maltzev,
and others—all these are factories which make railroads
out of shares. That is to say, they issue shares at a hundred
each, and people buy them for three hundred because they
pay "dividends." The more dividends, the better. And seeing as how no one knows a year in advance what dividends
will be declared, you have to play blind and buy, and keep
on buying. And that's how you get a rising market—that is,
the papers climb up, people make money, and me in the
middle. You should see, my dearest wife, how little people, petty brokers, poor devils, suddenly start growing
and become rich and powerful. They already sit in summer
cottages in Boiberik, go abroad to bathe in watering resorts; their ladies are smothered in velvet and gold; their

sons ride on bicycles; they keep governesses in their
homes; they talk French and play the piano; they eat pre-
serves and drink cherry brandy, and bother the cost! In
short, it's a good life, and all thanks to "papers"! When
daytime comes, you ought to see what goes on in Kreshchatik Street—it is simply alive with Jews! And no wonder. Offices are out-of-bounds to you; streets are not for
loitering—but can you help wanting to know how the exchange stands? So the streets are black with people, absolutely black! Today, for instance, word came from Petersburg that Putilov stands at one seventy-eight. So tell me,
how can you not buy Putilov? Or, for example, they are
saying that Maltzevs have already reached a thousand three
hundred fifty—so can anybody keep from buying them?
From day to day, they jump higher and higher! On my
Putilovs I already stand to make several hundreds, praise
the Lord! But with everybody chasing after them, catch me
selling them! On the contrary, I intend to buy a hundred
and fifty more Putilovs, some five Maltzevs, and several
Volgas, and if the Almighty comes to my aid, I'll also add a
few Transports, because they write from Petersburg: "For
heaven's sake, buy Transports!" Everybody here has Transports—men, women, doctors, teachers, doormen, servant
girls, laborers—is there anybody who hasn't got Transports? Whenever one Jew meets another, their first how-
do-you-do is: What's Transport doing today? You come
into a restaurant, the owner greets you with: "What's the
price of Transports today?" You go to buy a box of matches,
and the shopkeeper asks, "How high are Transports today?" . . . In a word, Yehupetz is really the place for
business. Everybody speculates, everybody rises in the
world, everybody makes money, and me in the middle.
And since I am pressed for time, I must cut this short.
Please God, in my next letter I'll write you everything in

detail. For the time being, may the Lord grant health and success. Give my kindest regards to everyone, to old and young, to big and small.

From me, your husband,
Menahem-Mendl.

J u s t   r e m e m b e r e d! As for your question about what I am doing in Boiberik at night, I thought I've already explained to you that Yehupetz is a city where Jews are not permitted to live unless they are merchants of the First Guild. After I know where I stand and what my portfolio amounts to, I'll buy myself a guild. Then I'll be able to live in Yehupetz like any other merchant. For the time being, I have to keep out of sight, and there's no better hiding place than Boiberik. Boiberik is simply a suburb with summer houses. There are lots of summer guests here. The summer guests keep running, so I run along with them—is it quite clear to you now?

As above.

4

Sheineh-Sheindl from Kasrilevka to her
husband, Menahem-Mendl, in Yehupetz

To my dear, esteemed, renowned, and honored husband,
the wise and learned Menahem-Mendl, may his light shine
forever.

In the first place, I want to let you know that
we are all, praise the Lord, perfectly well, and may we hear
the same from you, please God, and never anything worse.

In the second place, I am writing to say, my
dearest husband, that we've had a stroke of bad and good
luck, all in one. Our Moishe-Hersheli swallowed a kopeck!
I come home from the market—it was on a Friday—where
I bought some live fish—they were still twitching—and I
hear the child screaming to high heaven. I pinch him, I
pummel him—he doesn't stop yelling. "What do you want,
you little wretch, you miserable creature! Here, take all
my miseries, take a kopeck! Take a bellyache!" It was a job
to pacify him. A few minutes later, something jogs my
memory, and I ask, "Moishe-Hersheli, where is the kopeck?" "Ain't no topet," he says and points to his mouth.
He swallowed it?! Good heavens, what a calamity, what a
misfortune! I grab the child, pry his mouth open, and look
inside. Woe is me! "Moishe-Hersheli, my darling, my baby,
may I answer for every little bone of yours! Tell me, what
did you do with the kopeck?" I shake him; I hit him; I make
him black and blue—he keeps yelling and repeating, "No

59

topet! Hammm topet! Hammm!" To make a long story
short, I took him to the doctor, and the doctor told me to
feed him potatoes. For two whole days the poor child was
tortured and stuffed by force—not a drop of milk, not a
drop of water—potatoes, more potatoes, nothing but potatoes! I thought this would be the end of my child. On the
third day, I start tidying up the room, take a look under the
pillow on the bed—and would you believe it, the kopeck is
there!

Well, what do you say to those doctors? They know less
about sickness than I about miseries. There you are, as if I
haven't worries enough! As Mother says, God bless her,
"Today and tomorrow, there's always some sorrow. . . ." I
have to worry myself sick over his children, run to doctors
and all kinds of devils and sorcerers, while he, my gold
spinner—nothing worries him! He keeps flying from
Odessa to Yehupetz, and from Yehupetz to Boiberik!
What's all the excitement about? Oh, he found a treasure
trove: "Papers"! "Transports"! "Potfolios"! He talked it
into himself that one can get rich overnight. "The worst
sickness," Mother says, "is the one you talk yourself
into. . . ." You silly man, what fairy tales are you trying to
tell me? Stocks, smocks, dividends, reverends—they're not
worth an empty eggshell! Nobody has yet made a fortune
with five naked fingers. "If you sow a fever," Mother says,
"you'll reap a plague. . . ." Mendl, take heed of what I
say: All those wonderful Yehupetz folk of yours, who, as
you say, have suddenly become rich, will soon again, please
God, find their pockets full of nothing but air—only
maybe fresher air. . . . Because I believe in your "Ports"
and your "Malts" the way I believed in your Odessa's "London." I'd sooner believe in magic and witchcraft than all
your Yehupetz Potfolios. If a dog were to take a bite out of
my heart, it would go mad—that's how angry I get when I

see how other women are treated by their husbands. They have a right to put in a word sometimes. They are allowed to raise their voices, once in a while, high enough to make their husbands shake in their boots. Not like me, who must always speak gently, who daren't breathe a harsh word or utter a curse—and, despite all the shame I have to bear because of you, has to show a cheerful face to everybody. As Mother says, God bless her, "Pinch your cheeks to keep your complexion healthy." But how long, Mendl, how long? Am I made of stone? I am sure to pine away quietly—on my enemies' heads may it be—till I melt like a wax candle from sheer aggravation. Either I'll turn to water or else I'll burst, and may those loudmouths in your Yehupetz burst in my stead, which is the heartfelt wish of your really devoted wife, forever and amen,

Sheineh-Sheindl.

Oh, yes! Berl, your Uncle Menasheh's son, has had a new misfortune crash over his head. Last week his house burned down. He was left with the skin he was born in. And now there's a fine hullabaloo. His enemies informed against him. They claim everything he owned was insured at thrice its value, so it must have been he who prayed to Him "who commanded us to light the lights." . . . So he was summoned to the magistrate. But Berl wasn't born yesterday, either. He found witnesses who are going to swear that he wasn't at home that night. In the meantime, he is sitting in the lockup, and from fright, his Zlatke got birth pains and was delivered of a seven-months child. *Mazel tov!*

5

*Menahem-Mendl from Yehupetz to his wife,
Sheineh-Sheindl, in Kasrilevka*

To my dear, wise, and modest helpmeet, Sheineh-Sheindl,
long may she live!

F i r s t l y, I am come to inform you that I am, by the
grace of God, well and in good cheer. May the Lord,
blessed be His name, grant that we always hear from one
another none but the best, the most comforting, and the
happiest of tidings—amen.

A n d S e c o n d l y, I want you to know that I am already on my way to Warsaw. You'll probably want to know,
if I live in Yehupetz and deal with Petersburg, how do I
come to Warsaw? Don't worry—Warsaw is also quite a
town! Warsaw also has papers, and what papers! On Warsaw, speculators have made fortunes. Warsaw isn't Petersburg—Warsaw is spewing hundreds all around! Only last
week Warsaw went and raised Lilliputs from twelve hundred to two thousand. So I ask you, can you sit quietly and
not buy such a paper? Or take Railways for example. Some
time back—in fact only about three weeks ago—they stood
at fourteen hundred. Where do you think they are now? At
two thousand! And without the "coupon," too! Why, one
must be a criminal not to buy a Railway. There's another
advantage to Warsaw—she doesn't demand any cash; she
isn't interested in any deposits. You want Lilliputs? Rail-

ways? Just pay several hundred rubles to make up for the difference in exchange, and get yourself a "premium" until ultimo. In our language, all this means is: until the first of the month. And when the first of the month comes, you then have a choice—to accept the papers or not. But who'll let you wait till the first of the month? For that, brokers were created—so they shouldn't let you cross the street. "Maybe you've got some Lilliputs? Maybe you've got a few Railways?" This goes on till they offer you a quick profit and swindle you out of your papers. Only yesterday, for instance, two Odessa brokers got hold of me and stuck to me. They practically sat on me, coaxing me to give them my Lilliputs and Railways. They thought they found an easy customer. "Brothers!" I pleaded with them. "Let me alone! I haven't got any—I'm cleaned out—may I be as clean of sin!" In short, they clung so tight that they finally wheedled out of me my five Lilliputs and five Railways. On the other hand, I played a nice trick on them too. I covered my losses immediately by buying them right back— and so the papers remained with me! And I am quite confident that, please God, I'll double my profit, because lately, knock on wood, I've been having a wonderful streak of luck—whatever I buy today goes up tomorrow. Everybody says I was born lucky! If the good Lord grants that the Warsaw ultimo passes without a hitch, I'll clean out my entire portfolio and switch over to another office, because where I'm working now, there are, God forgive me, so many Jews milling around that you can't see what's black and what's white. Last week there was quite a big scandal. It almost came to blows—in fact, one of us got slapped in the face. . . . But since I am pressed for time, I must cut this short. Please God, in my next letter I'll write you everything in detail. For the time being, may the Lord grant health and success. Give my kindest regards to everybody, to old and young, to big and small.

From me, your husband,
Menahem-Mendl.

J u s t r e m e m b e r e d! As for Uncle Menasheh's son, Berl, I can very well believe the story; considering the kind of business possibilities Kasrilevka offers, no merchant could get along there differently. But with us in Yehupetz, you see, such a thing could never happen. First of all, everyone gets along fine here, knock on wood, and second, in case of fire, perish the thought, they have a special way to put it out: Before the flames start flickering, the fire brigade arrives in tin helmets; they jump right into the fire and pour water out of a hose. It would be worth your while to see a fire in Yehupetz!

As above.

6

*Sheineh-Sheindl from Kasrilevka to her
husband, Menahem-Mendl, in Yehupetz*

To my dear, esteemed, renowned, and honored husband,
the wise and learned Menahem-Mendl, may his light shine
forever.

In the first place, I want to let you know that
we are all, praise the Lord, perfectly well, and may we hear
the same from you, please God, and never anything worse.

In the second place, I am writing to say, my
dearest husband, that I believe you have really lost your
wits—probably the next thing you'll be doing is dancing
around the streets. It isn't enough for him that he is already known in Odessa, in Yehupetz, and in Boiberik! He's
got to have Warsaw know that there is a Menahem-Mendl
on the loose doing business in this world. Once upon a
time he dealt in London, and now he is dealing in used
horseshoes, last year's snow, scraps of papers, capers, japers
—and he has to go all the way to Warsaw in order to find
this sort of merchandise and even fight over it. Dear God
in heaven, if only there were a clever man who would
knock this silliness out of your head, to make you forget
about those dwarfs, or whatever their name is, and recall
that you have a wife till a hundred and twenty years, who
has to worry herself sick over his children, doing this for
them, doing that for them, day in, day out! Only yesterday
the baby was almost cooked to death by boiling water

poured through a sieve. Luckily it didn't scald the entire little head. As Mother says, God bless her, "Even in bad luck one has to be lucky. . . ." As for him—what does he care? He strolls about gaping at fires! What's so wonderful about that? Why, Yehupetz is burning! May it burn to an ash with Warsaw and Petersburg, all rolled in one, God in heaven! Anybody who believes in God simply bathes in my blood. Can I even cross a street? Everybody points a finger at me: "That's the one—Mrs. Menahem-Mendl of Yehupetz!" A fine name indeed, woe is me! But God bless Mother! She keeps repeating the same thing: No woman, she says, ought to let her husband out of her sight even for a minute because, she says, "The master's eye fattens the donkey. . . . It's easy to win, but it's hard to keep. . . ." She says, "I always knew no good would ever come of it. I hoped for a rich match," she says. "Well, how does that proverb go? Piggy, have you any money? Come to me and be my honey! . . . I wanted a pot of suet—well, the suet ran out, and the pot remained. . . . Would *I* be writing letters to him?" she says. "I'd write him a letter that would give him a fit, that's what I'd do! Whoever cannot take a hint," she says, "must be hit over the head with a stick. . . . If I were you," she says, "I'd bring him home on a broom! Or a poker!" Maybe you'll say she isn't right? But what can I do if I'm like a lamb—whatever you say is all right with me, and whatever you do, I agree to it. Any other woman in my shoes—Blumeh-Zlateh, for instance— would have been in Yehupetz a long time ago. She'd have seen all the rabbis and all the judges. She would have pounced on you in the middle of the street and given you such a lesson that you'd forget your name was Menahem-Mendl and that you're dealing in dwarfs. . . . I can judge your wonderful affairs and your riches by all the gifts you keep sending me from Yehupetz: the diamonds and the

pearls and the embroidered shifts and the woolen blankets
—yes, indeed! Look here, my dearest husband, I'm saying
this quite calmly: I cannot bear it any longer! Take your
choice: Either come home at once and start a normal life
like everyone else, or may my enemies perish and let there
be an end to all this, which is the heartfelt wish forever
and amen of your really devoted wife,

Sheineh-Sheindl.

7

Menahem-Mendl from Yehupetz to his wife,
Sheineh-Sheindl, in Kasrilevka

To my dear, wise, and modest helpmeet, Sheineh-Sheindl,
long may she live!

F i r s t l y, I am come to inform you that I am, by the
grace of God, well and in good cheer. May the Lord,
blessed be His name, grant that we always hear from one
another none but the best, the most comforting, and the
happiest of tidings—amen.

A n d S e c o n d l y, I want you to know that I am riding high; I am right above the clouds; I am on fire; I am
getting bigger and bigger! Lots of people envy me because
whatever I buy today goes up tomorrow. Railways have
gone up another two hundred, and my Lilliputs, praise the
Lord, are already on the other side of twenty-five hundred. But it still doesn't pay to sell, because everybody says
they're bound to go up and up. It stands to reason since all
Europe has pounced on our papers. They are organizing a
"syndicate" there—that means a combine. They want to
buy up every bit of paper to the last scrap. You'll probably
ask, whatever for? It's all very simple. Nowadays, you see,
there is a lot of money in the world; it simply rolls in the
streets. Interest rates are very low—four to five percent a
year is more than enough for us, and if it comes to ten-
fifteen percent, that's really something! As for Lilliputs
(not dwarfs as you call them) , I've already written you that

they are a kind of share in a factory which makes railroads and brings dividends. The railroads are in Siberia, the papers are in Warsaw, and the buyers are in Yehupetz—is it quite clear to you now? It's the same with Railways, Putilovs, and Transports. But if you think that when you buy papers, you can lay your eyes on them, you're mistaken again. Therefore, I've got to give you a clear picture of the business.

For example, you may feel like buying Transports. So you go to an office, hand something to the cashier as a deposit, and tell them to put you down for some merchandise. Then you get a receipt saying they bought for you so-and-so many Transports at such-and-such a price against such-and-such a deposit, and if, God forbid, it should go down, you have to bring them some more money. But of course, that's poppycock because it won't go down so quickly, and you won't have to bring any more money. It's the other way around; it keeps going up. That's how I've been working and, thank heaven, doing very well and, please God, I shouldn't do worse in the future.

If, God willing, I manage to tear myself away for a few days, I'd like to hop over to the city of Vasilkov and arrange a guild for myself; then I'll be able to save myself the trouble of wandering around—a Yehupetzite by day, a Boiberiker by night. Recently all the brokers have been transformed into legal merchants, and you ought to see how they live and what they eat, and what about their ladies with all their diamonds and pearls! I've already asked where one buys diamonds here, and I have an eye on several things for you, and believe me, not only in your Kasrilevka, but even in our Yehupetz, they'd make a splash! But since I am pressed for time, I must cut this short. Please God, in my next letter I'll write you everything in detail. For the time being, may the Lord grant health and success. My kindest greetings to everybody, to old and young, to big and small.

From me, your husband,
Menahem-Mendl.

Just remembered! You seem to think, my dearest wife, that I am the only pebble on the beach who deals in papers. Brodsky does, too. The difference is that when I go to buy papers, I have to measure the depth of my pocket, whereas when Brodsky buys papers, he takes a thousand in one shot, five thousand, ten thousand! That's Brodsky for you! When he rides in his carriage, all Kreshchatik trembles, all the Jews take their hats off, and me in the middle. Wouldn't it be nice if someday I became a Brodsky? . . . Everything is in the hands of God, my little goose. . . .

As above.

8

Sheineh-Sheindl from Kasrilevka to her
husband, Menahem-Mendl, in Yehupetz

To my dear, esteemed, renowned, and honored husband,
the wise and learned Menahem-Mendl, may his light shine
forever.

In the first place, I want to let you know that
we are all, praise the Lord, perfectly well, and may we
hear the same from you, please God, and never anything
worse.

In the second place, I am writing to say, my
dearest husband, that "one cannot make a silk purse out of
a sow's ear," as Mother says. . . . I say this in connection
with your precious sister-in-law, your Yentl, may she burn!
The other week she went to the trouble to spread a rumor
throughout the town that you went to America and threw
me over, may she never see the day, making me a widow
with yourself alive! What, according to her, put the idea in
her head? Sarah-Nehama heard it from Avrum's Leizer-
Hershke's own lips that Boruch-Benzion saw with his own
eyes a letter addressed to Moishe-Shmuel which Meir-
Mottl wrote from America. . . . So I run over to Moishe-
Shmuel: "Where is the letter?" Says he, "What letter?"
Say I, "The one Meir-Mottl wrote you from America."
Says he, "Who told you that?" Say I, "Boruch-Benzion."
Says he, "How could that liar and scandalmonger tell you
such a fairy tale when I haven't been on speaking terms

with him for over a year? . . ." So quite ready to burst, I run off to Boruch-Benzion and discover that he hasn't been in Kasrilevka for the past three weeks! Then I fly to Avrum's Leizer-Hershke and give him as good a piece of my mind as he deserves, for telling Sarah-Nehama a tale about a letter which was never written and never sent. So he stares at me as if I were out of my senses. What am I talking about? What am I dreaming about? It appears that the entire story was invented by her—your Yentl, may she pay for all our sins—she simply thought it up out of her head. Have you ever heard of such impudence?

But I suppose your mind isn't on the things I write about, because you are probably too busy with your Yehupetz ladies all hung with jewels, may they hang together with all their diamonds! Look here, Mendl, don't dare even mention them, I cannot bear to hear about them, I hate them so! I'm even sick of the gifts you intend to buy me there! I tell you in advance, my dearest husband, if you want to buy me a gift, get me something they don't wear in Yehupetz. I won't have you compare me with them, may they pay for my sins. But, I wouldn't mind if I finally got something from you in reality, not on paper. As Mother says, God bless her, "A few words less, a few bites more. . . ." Why put it off for the morrow, you silly man? In a business like yours, if you don't act in time, you'll be left with nothing! Say what you will, but until I see your dreams with my own eyes, I won't believe they exist. Not because, God forbid, I consider you a liar, but because you swallow as truth whatever those fine Yehupetz people tell you. And why do you compare yourself to Brodsky? Did you ever herd swine with him? . . . Can you get a bit of cash for your papers? Grab it, what are you waiting for?! Have the Odessa charlatans tracked you down to Boiberik and tried to swindle you out of your precious ware? They are welcome to it! The bargain is all theirs! As Mother says, "Gather the nuts in your hat and take to your heels. . . ." But why waste words on a madman? He has suddenly decided to become a merchant—and, what's more, a Vasilkov merchant! He has it so good that he cannot think of anything better. What's so attractive in Vasilkov? But it's no wonder—if by day one is a Yehupetzite, by night a Boiberiker, and affairs are carried out in Petersburg and Warsaw, in that case, one can become not only a Vasilkov merchant, but even a merchant in the land of Nod! Watch out, Mendl, lest with all your successes, I am forced to send you pocket money, God forbid, which is the heartfelt wish of your really devoted wife,

Sheineh-Sheindl.

I have a piece of news for you, my dearest husband—and I'm afraid it isn't good news. Your brother, Berl-Benyomin, has been left a widower. . . . Immediately I signed this letter, they came to tell me that Yentl died. She died in childbirth after giving birth to twins. The twins are alive, but she is dead. Seems to me it might have been the other way around. As Mother says, "The good Lord is right even when He acts on spite. . . ." Your sister-in-law—may she rest in the other world while I remain in mine—has always bickered with me, may she forgive me, but after all, she never trespassed on my property. Would it have made any difference to me if she had lived another hundred years and didn't leave seven little orphans behind, one smaller than the other? . . . I went to the funeral, and as a matter of fact, I cried so hard that I was half-dead by the time I came home. As Mother says, God bless her, "When one thinks of death, one isn't sure of life. . . ."

9

Menahem-Mendl from Yehupetz to his wife,
Sheineh-Sheindl, in Kasrilevka

To my dear, wise, and modest helpmeet, Sheineh-Sheindl,
long may she live!

F i r s t l y , I am come to inform you that I am, by the
grace of God, well and in good cheer. May the Lord,
blessed be His name, grant that we always hear from one
another none but the best, the most comforting, and the
happiest of tidings—amen.

A n d S e c o n d l y , I want you to know that I have
spent the entire week in Boïberik, in bed. It wasn't anything dangerous, God forbid, just a nasty accident. I fell on
my back, I couldn't turn from side to side, but it's a little
better now. All week long I thought I'd go out of my mind
—it's no joke to be cut off from the stock market for eight
whole days, without knowing how the exchange is going. I
kept imagining that everything was topsy-turvy there. God
willing, tomorrow or the day after, I'll certainly go back to
the city. In the meantime, I am writing you a letter because I feel like having a chat with you, and by the way
give you a full account about where I'm at, so you shouldn't
think I got mixed up in anything, God forbid, got involved or swindled.

My portfolio now contains a total of a hundred and fifty
Putilovs, a hundred Transports, five Maltzevs, five Lilliputs, and five Railways—besides the premiums. Well, I've

already sold the Putilovs and the Transports in advance (on a three-ruble deposit), and as soon as they buy them up from me—and they are sure to buy them up—after deducting all expenses, I'll have a clear profit of four to five thousand rubles. Besides this, I have a couple of dozen baisses in Putilov and Maltzev—all on Class A confirmations—and I figure on clearing another seventeen to eighteen hundred on them. You now have a good total of seven thousand rubles almost. The five Maltzevs I reckon at four thousand at the very worst, because it would be a shame, a disgrace, if they didn't rise soon to at least two thousand apiece, even if they did take a slight dip lately; but that's only due to the tricks of the Petersburg swindlers who are trying to cover themselves up. What remains, then, is the top of the cream: I mean, the Lilliputs and the Railways; here the arithmetic is simple and clean like gold: Until the ultimo we still have a good eighteen days to go, and since Lilliputs are going up at the rate of a hundred a day, you have a sure profit of $18 \times 100 \times 5$ shares, which adds up to exactly nine thousand, and not a shekel less. And what about the Railways? They are jumping up at the rate of a hundred and fifty a day—which makes $18 \times 150 \times 5$—and doesn't that add up to thirteen thousand five hundred? And how about Volga, Dnieper, Don, and all the other rivers? . . .

In a word, I haven't yet ordered an outsize purse for my coat, but after all expenses (such as brokers' fees, swindlers' commissions, etc.) are deducted, the total should be close to forty-fifty thousand! If, God willing, the ultimo passes without a hitch, I will, please the Lord, realize on all my papers and make an about-face. It means I'll start with baisses, sell everything, and make money on the other side. After a while I'll again swing over to hausses and again make a fat bundle. So, the good Lord willing, the fifty thousand can become a hundred thousand; the hundred thousand, two hundred thousand; and so on, up to a million. How else, you silly goose, can you become a rich man, a Brodsky? And what is Brodsky after all? Flesh and blood who eats and drinks and sleeps. I've seen Brodsky with my own eyes, may they always enjoy such a pleasant sight. . . .

In a word, you are not to worry, my dearest wife. I've looked into this business of speculation, studied it thoroughly, and I've become such a wizard on the stock exchange that people now come to me for advice, if you please! With God's help, I do understand the game. And the fact that you have no faith in me and tell me to quit doesn't surprise me. What about Hinkes? There's a speculator here called Hinkes, a very hot speculator and a terrific gambler. By day he plays the stock market, and by night he plays cards, and this is what happened to him. One night only a week ago he saw a bad card in a dream, a sure sign of baisse, so he went off to Petersburg and Warsaw at once and cleared out his entire portfolio in a single day. You can imagine that the poor fellow is now tearing his hair out. Well, it serves him right—he shouldn't believe in dreams!

I can hardly wait till tomorrow to find out how the market stands. I've decided that the minute I get to town, I'll make a beeline to the jeweler for your brooch and the diamond earrings, and if I only have time enough, I'll hop over to the Podol District to buy you some linen, tablecloths, towels, and material for children's underwear, and maybe a few other things for the house. So it's not like you say that I have forgotten all about you, God forbid. And since I am pressed for time, I must cut this short. Please God, in my next letter I'll write you everything in detail. For the time being, may the Lord grant health and success. Greet the children, God bless them, and give my kindest regards to your father and mother, to old and young, to big and small. And please tell Berl-Benyomin for me that he shouldn't take it to heart. A wife is the gift of God—the Lord gave, and the Lord has taken away.

From me, your husband,
Menahem-Mendl.

J u s t   r e m e m b e r e d! From what you say about Vasilkov, I see you didn't understand me at all. Since I am not allowed to live here, I want to become a local merchant—and that can be arranged only by getting registered in Vasilkov for at least half a year. As soon as I obtain a permit to live in Yehupetz, I shall, please God, rent an apartment for you in the Podol District and bring you and the children here, blessed be the day. And your being so set against Yehupetz is simply because you don't know the city and its people. As far as the city is concerned—no need to waste words, it's a doll. And the people here, they are simply silver and gold. How does it compare to Odessa?! Here everyone is so kind and easygoing, men and women alike. They have only one weakness: They like a card game. The moment it is dark, they get down to work: They sit themselves down till daybreak and shout, "Pass!" The big shots play a game called Preference, and the smaller fry play Knock-Knock, Points, and Turtle-Myrtle.

As above.

10

Sheineh-Sheindl from Kasrilevka to her
husband, Menahem-Mendl, in Yehupetz

To my dear, esteemed, renowned, and honored husband, the wise and learned Menahem-Mendl, may his light shine forever.

In the first place, I want to let you know that we are all, praise the Lord, perfectly well, and may we hear the same from you, please God, and never anything worse.

In the second place, I am writing to say, my dearest husband, that you needn't stay in mourning any longer. I can congratulate you! Your fine brother, your Berl-Benyomin, the widower, has already remarried, blessed be the day! He didn't even have the patience to wait two whole months. He went off to the city of Berdichev, which seems to keep the whole world supplied with stepmothers, and brought from there a new mother for his children—a nineteen-year-old girl, if you please! How does that look?! Well, you men don't get more than you deserve. As Mother says, God bless her, "It's better for us to become widows than to have you make orphans of our children. . . ." I can just imagine your tears, Mendl, if you should, God forbid, outlive me—may the Yehupetz ladies never live to see the day! The thirty days of mourning wouldn't be over before they'd swarm over you like wasps and try to snap you up! And as Mother says: "Her loss is his gain. . . ." And then you could remain in Yehupetz forever. . . .

You say, Mendl, that you are flying high. All right, keep flying! Spread your wings! Jump right into the fire! But don't expect me to come to you, even if I knew you were on your deathbed! And your fifty thousand don't scare me either. First of all, you are mine, with or without fifty thousand. And second, I don't give a fig for your fifty thousand. As Mother says, God bless her, "So long as the money is on paper, it's nothing but paper. . . ." To be frank, my dearest husband, if you can count on a few stray shekels and are waiting till you collect a round fifty thousand, you are either a madman or a scoundrel, a criminal, a murderer who has no thought for your wife till one hundred and twenty years or for your children. I like the way he feeds me on tomorrows! Tomorrow he'll go to the jeweler; tomorrow he'll buy me linen—everything tomorrow! Fool that you are, let the good Lord take care of tomorrow. Do the buying today. Cash in now; grab at once—it will be as good as found! My mother, may she enjoy a long and healthy life, says very wisely, "Daughter, what good are gifts to you—tablecloths, pillow slips? Money—that's what he ought to send!" She says, "The angel of death doesn't ask the corpse whether it has a shroud. . . ." I'll wait another two weeks or so till I feel quite well again, and then, God willing, I'll get into a carriage and go after you. I don't envy you then! I'll hound you at every step, I'll follow you everywhere. And I promise you that you'll flee from that city in the middle of the night, which is the heartfelt wish of your really devoted wife,

Sheineh-Sheindl.

I I

Menahem-Mendl from Yehupetz to his wife,
Sheineh-Sheindl, in Kasrilevka

To my dear, wise, and modest helpmeet, Sheineh-Sheindl,
long may she live!

F i r s t l y, I am come to inform you that I am, by the
grace of God, well and in good cheer. May the Lord,
blessed be His name, grant that we always hear from one
another none but the best, the most comforting, and the
happiest of tidings—amen.

A n d S e c o n d l y, I want you to know, my dearest
wife, that the end of the world has come! The rates of exchange which arrived from Petersburg are so terrible that
everything went dark before our eyes. It hit us like a bolt
of lightning, like a bomb! All the offices are deserted;
Kreshchatik was hit by an earthquake. And right on the
heels of Petersburg came Warsaw, which also dashed down
its rates of exchange! Such a hullabaloo, an uproar, a panic
and confusion! The speculators have fled, disappeared into
thin air, and me in the middle. The stock market is finished!
The brokers' offices are standing empty; the bankers are
worried—it's like the destruction of the Temple! Just imagine, my dearest wife, the Maltzev shares which I considered dirt cheap at two thousand suddenly decided to drop
to nine hundred and fifty. Or take Putilov, for example—
sooner would I have expected them to rot than to fall from
one hundred and eighty to sixty-seven! No need to men-

tion Transport. Transport may as well be shoveled into a grave—nobody wants to touch them! The same with Volga, Don, and the other papers. But all this is a picnic compared with Warsaw. Warsaw is the ruin of us all! From the day the world was created, there hasn't been such a massacre as in Warsaw. Warsaw decided to beat Lilliputs from two thousand four hundred and fifty down to six hundred and twenty! And what of the Railways? They were holding their own so well, we were expecting them to reach three thousand any minute. And where do you think they are now? You'll never guess: at a wretched four hundred! What do you say to such a market? It's the end of the world! Poor Warsaw! It will never recover from shame; it kept pushing up and up and up, and all of a sudden such a merry-go-round! What is the cause of this somersault, nobody knows. Some say this; others say that. It's all because of money—I mean, shortage of money. In German it's called *Geldmangel*, and in our language it's simply *out of pocket*. You'll probably say, how come? Wasn't it only yesterday that money was rolling in the streets? . . . There you've got me! Nobody can answer that one. But whatever it is, all the speculators have been burned, and me in the middle.

To tell you the truth, I'm not so sore about Petersburg as about Warsaw. After all, Petersburg wasn't anything much. It's been sliding down quietly; it dropped twenty rubles a day, thirty rubles, and that's all; it is, one might say, businesslike. But Warsaw! May it burst! It treated us like Sodom, perish the thought! Not a day passes without Warsaw ripping off one hundred and fifty rubles, two hundred rubles, three hundred rubles, one blow after another, without giving us a chance to come to our senses! Millions that city of Warsaw has cost us, millions! Good heavens, where was our common sense? If I had only listened to

you, my dearest wife, I would now be thumbing my nose
over and over again at the whole world. Even Brodsky
couldn't compare with me! But I suppose it was the will of
God. Evidently, my turn has not come yet. . . .

One lucky thing is that at least my banker, God bless
him, is not pressing me for the few shekels I owe him. In
fact, he is even sorry for me. He says, when things take a
turn for the better, he'll try to push something my way to
earn a little money on. . . . But for the time being, there's
nothing to do. On the exchange, it isn't speculators you see
wandering about; it's ghosts. Brokers loiter around kicking
their heels. Everything is dark and bitter. Speculation is
dead, they say—it will never come back to life. There's
nothing to lay one's hand on. If my pockets weren't so
empty, I could drift along for a while, till the bad times
are over. The sky, as the saying goes, hasn't dropped on the
earth yet. Stuff and nonsense! I feel it in my heart that
there will still be something to do. God is eternal, and
Yehupetz is a city. If it isn't one thing, it'll be another. . . .

But where to get a little hard cash? As your mother says,
"If you haven't any fingers, you cannot thumb your
nose. . . ." I've tried to encourage a couple of men to give
me a small loan for a short time, but they swear there is
such a shortage of money in town that even the big fellows
are hard pressed and practically flat on their faces, pinched
for every penny. I wish to heaven the good Lord would
send me a miracle: a gang of robbers to kill me, or I should
just drop dead in the middle of the street because, my dearest wife, I can't stand it any longer! How did this happen
to me?! I was doing so well! I had, as the saying goes, pockets bursting at the seams—and all of a sudden, where am
I? . . . And since I am terribly depressed, I must cut this
short. Please God, in my next letter I'll write you everything in detail. For the time being, may the Lord grant

health and success. Write me what the children are doing, God bless them, and how you are feeling, and give my kindest greetings to your mother and father, to old and young, to big and small.

From me, your husband,
Menahem-Mendl.

J u s t r e m e m b e r e d! There is an old saying: "After your house burns down, you're bound to get rich." I believe that's true, and after the kind of catastrophe we've had here, one could do wonderful business. Because everything has become dirt cheap. One can now make hausses with premiums on the best shares, almost free of charge. I venture to predict, and I'm willing to wager my head on it, that whoever goes to Petersburg or Warsaw now and buys something will find luck there! For after all, I can really claim that I have the hang of this game at my fingertips. For speculation you need only three things: brains, luck, and money. As for brains—praise God, I have as much as any speculator here. As for luck—that's in the hands of the Almighty. And money? Money is in Brodsky's pocket.

As above.

12

*Sheineh-Sheindl from Kasrilevka to her
husband, Menahem-Mendl, in Yehupetz*

To my dear, esteemed, renowned, and honored husband,
the wise and learned Menahem-Mendl, may his light shine
forever.

In the first place, I want to let you know that
we are all, praise the Lord, perfectly well, and may we hear
the same from you, please God, and never anything worse.

In the second place, I am writing to say, my
dearest husband, that actually I ought to write you a lot,
but I have nothing to write you, as I've run out of sup-
plies. Anyhow, what good will it do me to dig your grave,
God forbid, and bury you alive? Would that be of any use
to me? After all, I am not Blumeh-Zlateh who enjoys nag-
ging her husband; I am not going to nag you. I am not going to utter one harsh word to you. I won't even open my
mouth. I will only ask you one single question, and may
my enemies pay for all my sins. Tell me, didn't I warn you it
would be like this? Tell me, didn't I keep writing you all
the time: Run, Mendl, run for your life!? What good are
old rags, I say, what good are scraps of papers? As Mother
says, "If you stay at home, you'll never wear out your
boots. . . ." But he wouldn't listen to me! He got stuck
in his Yehupetz! He's crazy about all those wonderful people there—may they all go crazy in your stead and mine
and for all Israel before I ever stretch out my hand to

them for a loan, may the good Lord stretch them out with a
light plague and a summer fever to last the year! How does
Mother say, God bless her? "Better reach the end of a
prayer than reach out for the help of a man. . . ."

I cannot make you out, Mendl. You know very well that
it says in the holy books, "Man is born against his will and
dies against his will." So why talk all that nonsense? Everything comes from God. You can see for yourself that the
Almighty is simply punishing you for coveting fried birds
of paradise, easy profits in Yehupetz! A Jew has to work by
the sweat of his brow and provide bread for his wife! Take
Nehemia—he's also a fine, lettered young man who knows
a thing about books—may I know as much happiness! And
yet just see how he wears himself to the bone. He attends
every fair; he trudges on foot; he tills the soil and works
like a donkey—all for his wife. Maybe he too would prefer
to strut around Yehupetz like you, swinging a cane, never
lifting a finger, dealing in old rags and bottles; maybe he
too would like to go off to Boiberik and ogle the ladies of
Yehupetz while they play their pretty card games. But
Nehemia has a wife of his own who is called *Blumeh-
Zlateh*. All Blumeh-Zlateh has to do is give Nehemia one
look, and he loses the power of speech. He understands
the slightest flutter of her eyelid. On the contrary, let him
try, for example, to return from a fair without bringing her
some gift—a nice coat, a little hat, a pretty umbrella, or
whatever aches and plagues she may set her heart on. You
think she is like me, who has to be satisfied with letters telling me every time that you're buying me this and getting
me that—and in the end, it's all gone with the wind? But I
suppose you think I'm dying for your gifts? I need them
like a toothache—all these brooches and diamonds of
yours, so long as I live to see you in the flesh, hale and
hearty! I no longer believe you are alive. Tonight I saw

Grandmother Zeitl in a dream, may she rest in peace—exactly as she used to look, not a bit different. That's why I can't wait till I finally see you alive and as soon as possible, which is the heartfelt wish of your really devoted wife,

Sheineh-Sheindl.

Book III
MILLIONS
Merchants, Brokers, and Speculators

I

Menahem-Mendle from Yehupetz to his wife,
Sheineh-Sheindl, in Kasrilevka

To my dear, wise, and modest helpmeet, Sheineh-Sheindl,
long may she live!

F i r s t l y, I am come to inform you that I am, by the
grace of God, well and in good cheer. May the Lord,
blessed be His name, grant that we always hear from one
another none but the best, the most comforting, and the
happiest of tidings—amen.

A n d S e c o n d l y, I want you to know that I am no
longer a speculator. I spit on speculation—may all Jews
avoid it like the plague! It wore me out like a fever, it
made me old and gray. What we endured here is no joke.
It's all over with Yehupetz; the exchange is upside down;
there's darkness everywhere—it's like after a war—even
worse, perish the thought, than it was in Odessa! Everybody is done for and panic-stricken. People have taken to
bankruptcy, and me in the middle. Every day, another de-
faulter. Bankruptcy has become very much in fashion.
And what's more, the important bankers, the big shots,
have started to make themselves scarce. In the van was
the banker through whom we all used to handle with
Petersburg and Warsaw. One bright morning I came to his
office where I was stuck with some Maltzevs and several
Putilov shares for which *he* was to get a small "difference"
from *me*. I started asking around where he might be, our

fine lord. So they tell me he departed, God rest his soul—
he's already in America! In short, there started a hue and
cry, there was a rush to the iron safe, but nothing was
found in it except a bottle of ink and an old worn-out coin
—with a hole in it, besides. . . . Another banker left a
collection of Jewish calendars in his safe beginning with
the year 1873 up to the present day, and he himself made
off to Palestine. A third one—and a very big banker indeed
—did not default but was simply plucked to the tune of
several millions in a single week and was left with nothing
but his good name. Only Brodsky somehow managed to
scramble out of the mess by a miracle.

So I thought it over and came to the conclusion that
if it isn't in the books, no amount of brains will do any
good. At any rate, it's lucky I took a look around on time
and managed to throw myself into a new job—and a most
respectable job, too. That is to say, I have now become a
broker—simply a broker, in fact, a broker right here in
Yehupetz on the stock exchange. There are as many brokers
in Yehupetz, knock on wood, as stars in the sky—so why
should I be any worse than they? Haven't I also got hands
and feet and a nose and eyes, just like any other Jew? Char-
acters as wellborn as I are aplenty here—and yet none con-
siders himself too good to take his cane in hand and start
on brokerage. Is it such a difficult science, come to think of
it? As long as you know how to tell a lie and, on top of it,
possess a good stock of impudence, anybody can become a
broker. Quite to the contrary, the more lies and the greater
impudence, the better the broker! Believe me, in Yehupetz there are some brokers who in your Kasrilevka
would be good only as servants or coachmen—they hardly
know how to sign their names, and yet you can see for
yourself—as your mother says, "If it were the will of God,
you'd shoot fire from a rod. . . ." All you have to do is put

on a white shirt and a nice hat and start creeping, snooping, sniffing, eavesdropping—a jump here, a bounce there, and: "My commission, if you please!" Commission in brokers' language is hush money. And oh, how sweet is commission money! You earn it without a headache, without a pain in your stomach. Why, only yesterday, I picked up a fifty in commission, and may you and I know a pain and an ache, if I know what I got it for! I made several tons of sugar with ease—easier than smoking a cigarette. That is to say, the sugar was made by other people—I simply found myself in the middle of the deal. In short, with God's help, I made a fifty! And, please God, in about a year's time, I'll get back on my feet again and become what I used to be, because with us in Yehupetz, money plays first fiddle. A human being is not worth a straw—his origins, his ancestry, have no value at all. You may be anything and nothing—so long as you have money! And since I'm very busy and pressed for time, I must cut this short. Please God, in my next letter, I'll write you everything in detail. For the time being, may the Lord grant health and success. Greet the children, God bless them, and give my kindest greetings to your father and mother, to old and young, to big and small.

From me, your husband,
Menahem-Mendl.

Just remembered! Please write me what's new at home. Has it been raining? How are the beets getting on, and are there many beetles? Let me know as soon as possible because this is very important for me!

As above.

2

Sheineh-Sheindl from Kasrilevka to her
husband, Menahem-Mendl, in Yehupetz

To my dear, esteemed, renowned, and honored husband,
the wise and learned Menahem-Mendl, may his light shine
forever.

In the first place, I want to let you know that
we are all, praise the Lord, perfectly well, and may we hear
the same from you, please God, and never anything worse.

In the second place, I am writing to say, my
dearest husband, my darling, my sweet one—may an epi-
demic sweep all my enemies away! You villain, you mon-
ster, you scoundrel, you know very well that your wife is on
her deathbed after the reparation which that wonderful
doctor made on me—I wish it on all your Yehupetz ladies!
The result is I can hardly drag my feet. And all the trouble I'm having with your children, with their teeth, their
tonsils, their stomachs, their diphtherias, and all the other
plagues on my enemies' heads! How could you remain si-
lent all this time and not even send a letter? Make up your
mind: Either you are dead—so write and tell me so—or
else you are alive—then you certainly ought to write! But
what's the use of talking to a dolt? As Mother says, long
may she live, "Sooner will a sot turn sober than a fool turn
wise. . . ." Just imagine, woe is me! Sheineh-Sheindl,
Boruch-Hirsh and Lea-Dvossi's daughter, has to have a

broker for a husband! But naturally, becoming a broker or
a bun peddler or a dog catcher—anything is worthwhile so
long as one remains in Yehupetz, may it sink through the
ground! Here you write you've picked up a fifty at that
beautiful new job of yours, and you expect to pick up a
fifty every day. Not every Monday is Purim. So you think
it's as Odessa used to be, with "London," "papers,"
"dwarfs," and the rest of your previous successes which are
sticking in my gullet to this day? You silly man, your eyes
will pop out of your head fifty times before you live to see
another fifty! Besides, I have no faith in your Yehupetz
affairs, which always start out with such a bounce and end
up with the bottom falling out.

And as for what you write about being glad you haven't
lost your mind, I must say I can't see it from the things you
write—they make no sense at all. You ask about beets and
whether it's raining in our parts. What do you expect—
snow in midsummer? And what have menfolk got to do
with beets anyhow? And where can you get beets this time
of the year? In our parts we've been cooking soup from
cucumbers or sorrel—beets don't appear on the market till
the autumn holidays! And what's all this about beetles?
What do you need beetles for? Haven't we enough trouble
from bedbugs? I ask you! You live in Yehupetz; you make
sugar; you pick up fifties—so why do you need beets, rains,
and beetles on top of it all? Is that some new kind of merchandise? But Mother, may she really live long, says very
wisely, "A madman breaks his neighbor's windows, never
his own. . . ." So listen to me, Mendl, drop all this rubbish, and if you still have anything left over from that fifty,
hurry up and come home! If not, I'll send you something
for the journey. Remember, you have a wife till a hundred
and twenty years and little children who are waiting for

you day in, day out, and let people stop gossiping about me, and let my face stop burning, which is the heartfelt wish of your really devoted wife,

Sheineh-Sheindl.

Oh, yes! Why don't you ask what's new at home? Evidently it doesn't matter to you in the least that my mother has broken up my little sister's engagement! Do you think it was over money? Money, of course, is a separate matter— but it all started when the young man's father came to visit us on Sabbath, and Mother had some words with him. She hinted that he is descended from butchers and said something to the effect that one can expect nothing but beef from an ox—and other little digs of that nature. So home he went, a plague on him, he returned the betrothal contract, and in the meantime, poor Nehame-Braindl is for the third time "a bride no longer and a spinster again."

3

Menahem-Mendl from Yehupetz to his wife,
Sheineh-Sheindl, in Kasrilevka

To my dear, wise, and modest helpmeet, Sheineh-Sheindl,
long may she live!

F i r s t l y , I am come to inform you that I am, by the
grace of God, well and in good cheer. May the Lord,
blessed be His name, grant that we always hear from one
another none but the best, the most comforting, and the
happiest of tidings—amen.

A n d S e c o n d l y , I want you to know, my dearest
wife, that you haven't quite digested what I wrote to you.
You are not to worry about my changing over from a speculator into a broker—that's only for the best. I am not the
only one in Yehupetz. Here we have, knock on wood,
plenty of brokers—sugar brokers, stockbrokers, wheat
brokers, money brokers, brokers for houses, estates, forests, machinery, rafts, wooden beams, factories, refineries, railways. . . . Whatever one's lips can name and one's
heart may desire, there's a broker for it. . . . No business
is done here without a broker. And every broker needs another broker, because *this* one has a buyer, and *that* one
has a seller—and together they make a good match. Also, it
sometimes happens that two or three other brokers get
hold of the first two brokers, and then they all share the
commission equally. And if they cannot agree on the
shares, they either resort to arbitration or settle it the

Odessa way: They compromise with blows. . . . Is the brokerage business clear to you now?

The biggest of all are the sugar brokers because all the sugar passes through their hands, so they are making fortunes, ride around in their own carriages, live in summer cottages in Boiberik, play cards, and keep mistresses and cabaret singers. . . . Generally speaking, I've decided that brokerage is the best possible trade, for what risk does a broker run? Figure it out for yourself: If I am lucky, my client will make money; if not, we'll both eat dust!

As you say, it is quite true one doesn't pick up a fifty every day. After that first deal, I have made nothing more so far, and the first fifty has melted away in the twinkling of an eye because I was so much in debt that I did not even own the hair on my head, and besides I lent a few shekels here and there so now I am again without a kopeck. But, on the other hand, I hope, please God, to close a new deal soon, and then I'll send you several shekels by check.

And as for my question about rains, it's all very simple. You know, of course, that sugar is made out of beets, and beets have to have rain—otherwise, they won't grow. That is why I asked you whether it's been raining. God grant there is no rain at all so the beetles can gorge themselves sick to the stomach on beets, because if there are no beets, there won't be any sugar, and when there is no sugar, it's worth its weight in gold—then speculators can make business, brokers can earn money, and me in the middle. And since I am very busy and pressed for time, I must cut this short. For the time being, may the Lord grant health and success. Greet the children, God bless them, and give my kindest regards to everyone, to old and young, to big and small.

From me, your husband,
Menahem-Mendl.

Just remembered! As for your sister, if she hasn't become engaged again, I've got a match for her—but something extra special. He's a local fellow, a bachelor, as a matter of fact—though not a very young one (actually he is well on in years and has gray hairs in his beard). He isn't wealthy either. But he has a good trade. He is a broker, and he fiddles with sugar. This party would be just the thing for your sister because he is a very decent, quiet fellow. If you like the idea, dash off a telegram to me, or else send a postcard, and I'll arrange for them to meet.

As above.

4

*Sheineh-Sheindl from Kasrilevka to her
husband, Menahem-Mendl, in Yehupetz*

To my dear, esteemed, renowned, and honored husband,
the wise and learned Menahem-Mendl, may his light shine
forever.

In the first place, I want to let you know that
we are all, praise the Lord, perfectly well, and may we hear
the same from you, please God, and never anything worse.

In the second place, I am writing to say, my
dearest husband, that may all the bad dreams I've had last
night, tonight, and throughout the year be inflicted on my
enemies! Wasn't that simply wonderful news—if it doesn't
rain, there won't be any beets; if there aren't any beets,
there won't be any sugar; and if there is no sugar, then he'll
make money! "If ifs and ans were pots and pans. . . ."
And what if I were to give you the good news that every
single day it's been pouring cats and dogs here, and the
beets are growing faster than weeds, and there isn't a
single insect in sight except for bedbugs and cockroaches
—will that make you feel better?

God is my witness, I felt it in my bones that not even a
shadow has remained of that fifty! I knew beforehand you'd
squander the money on loans before you'd recall that you
have a wife till a hundred and twenty years. Loans? If I
were you, I'd give those people all my troubles on loan,
because when the time comes for *you* to ask them for a

loan, you'll find nobody at home. As Mother says, God
bless her, "A taker is never a giver, and friendship doesn't
go as far as the pocket. . . ." But who is to blame, except
myself? It serves me right for always giving in to you! All
that luxury has turned his head! He runs around his precious Yehupetz like a baron, and he's only short of rain and
beets, while I have to lead a dog's life, with terrible bad
luck following me at every step! I have a child called
Moishe-Hersheli—so he falls down and splits open his lip!
I have a ring with little stones—so the servant girl steals
it! Troubles come, knock on wood, from every side; as
Mother says, God bless her, "When good luck is in sight,
you can empty the slop pail. . . ."

Well, was I wrong when I told you that not every Monday is Purim and fifties don't clutter up the streets? And as
for that wonderful match you propose for Nehame-Braindl,
he can stew in his own juice—that old bachelor of yours
with his gray beard. Yehupetz won't live to see us make a
match in that city. Do you know whom they are offering to
her? Her very first fiancé all over again. He has already
managed to divorce his first wife, and now he's after my
little sister again. Seems she's taken his fancy, that charla-
tan! But as Mother says, God bless her, "Better your own
thief than a strange rabbi. . . ." And as soon as the betrothal is settled, the wedding will take place, and just try
not to come to Nahame-Braindl's wedding, which is the
heartfelt wish of your really devoted wife,

Sheineh-Sheindl.

Our Koppel has turned the trick again—he went bank-
rupt, dropped about three hundred rubles, and is now
again in good standing in town. And Uncle Menasheh's
son Berl has again had a calamity: another fire in his

house, to the tune of a hundred rubles maybe, and he has received two hundred and fifty in insurance. But I think this will be the last fire in our town since it is expected that the Anchor Insurance Company will refuse to accept insurance on Jewish houses and shops in Kasrilevka. And Miriam-Beile has thought up a new one—what does she need a wig for? She prefers to parade bareheaded beneath the sky! She is copying our Mr. Rich Man's daughter-in-law, that hussy who plays cards with young men. But I don't like to gossip. As Mother says, God bless her, "If you see a mote in your neighbor's eye, you're bound to miss the beam in your own. . . ." And in heaven's name, write me at once what are "mistresses" and "cabaret singers." What do you need them for?

5

Menahem-Mendl from Yehupetz to his wife,
Sheineh-Sheindl, in Kasrilevka

To my dear, wise, and modest helpmeet, Sheineh-Sheindl,
long may she live!

F i r s t l y , I am come to inform you that I am, by the
grace of God, well and in good cheer. May the Lord,
blessed be His name, grant that we always hear from one
another none but the best, the most comforting and the
happiest of tidings—amen.

A n d S e c o n d l y , I want you to know that your guess
was correct. Sugar is really no business for me. First of all,
because it's too hard to hold one's own among the big sugar
brokers; before you can make a move, the biggest sugar
broker pounces and snatches the deal from under your
nose even though he is a big shot—and just try and go to
court about it! And if you should ask, how is that? Where is
justice? Well, you may as well know: In Yehupetz one
doesn't ask such questions. Justice is not one of the coins in
circulation in Yehupetz! There is no compassion here, and
there is no justice. That is number one. Number two—I
ask you: What kind of business is this sugar business if
you have to keep your eyes glued to the sky all day long and
pray to God that today it should rain, and tomorrow it
shouldn't? . . .

In short, I've come to the conclusion that the game is not
for me: You have to have tremendous impudence, disre-

gard the calendar, tell lies, talk speculators into believing
that they don't know chalk from cheese, and keep talking
until they get sick of listening and are driven into cold
sweat. . . . God alone knows, I haven't got it in me. I
like to earn my shekel honestly. Please God, I've now got a
business which I know is a business. That is to say, I am
lending money on a percentage basis. This is called dis-
counting. I lend and borrow money against promissory
notes. In other words, I redeem anybody's promissory notes
at a rather paltry discount, for, as the saying goes, "Earn
less, so long as you sleep sound. . . ." It's the kind of business which gains respect for you everywhere, because people who need hard cash urgently become as soft as butter:
They crawl and cringe and promise the broker mountains
of gold. . . . For instance, the good Lord has sent me a
storekeeper from Berdichev who trades in dry goods. I got
to know him at the rooming house where I am staying. He
is an exceptional young man with a golden heart. He promises that if I get him credit of ten to twenty thousand shekels, he'll give me such a reward that I'll be able to drop
brokerage altogether. . . . Although for the time being
I haven't managed to raise a kopeck for him, I have every
hope, please God, that I'll soon raise it for certain. . . .

Any broker who is close to money lives high and rides in
his own carriage. You have to realize that here in our
Yehupetz a horse and carriage command more respect than
men. . . . And since I am busy and pressed for time, I
must cut this short. Please God, in my next letter I shall
write you everything in detail. For the time being, may
the Lord grant health and success. Greet the children, God
bless them, and give my kindest regards to your father and
mother, to old and young, to big and small.

From me, your husband,
Menahem-Mendl.

Just remembered! As for Koppel's catastrophe, you simply make me laugh when I compare it to the bankruptcies here! Any merchant who hasn't defaulted at least three times is not even considered a merchant. Formerly it used to be fashionable to take to one's heels after a bankruptcy. This is no longer in fashion. It isn't even called bankruptcy here—simply nonpayment. In other words—the man doesn't want to pay, so go do him something! . . . As for your asking about the meaning of mistresses and cabaret singers, in the holy tongue they are called concubines. But I give you my word of honor that as far as I'm concerned, it goes into one ear and comes out of the other. . . .

As above.

6

Sheineh-Sheindl from Kasrilevka to her husband, Menahem-Mendl, in Yehupetz

To my dear, esteemed, renowned, and honored husband, the wise and learned Menahem-Mendl, may his light shine forever.

In the first place, I want to let you know that we are all, praise the Lord, perfectly well, and may we hear the same from you, please God, and never anything worse.

In the second place, I am writing to say, my dearest husband, that as true as I live, your sweet little letters are going to make my heart burst, may a bomb burst in the breasts of all my enemies! Here I was thinking that you were making sugar—and suddenly you go and turn into a moneylender! Where did you get money to lend out? If the Almighty was so good as to help you out with a few rubles, does it follow that you have to scatter them immediately to the winds? Didn't you yourself write me not so very long ago that as soon as a bit of money comes your way, you'll send it to me at once by check? Is that how you keep your promises? But Mother, God bless her, was right after all. She says to me, "My daughter, don't expect a single kopeck from there, because nothing ever comes back from the cemetery, and," she says, "especially from that wonderful town of Yehupetz, may it burn to an ash. You know the old saying: 'Don't look to a drone for honey!' . . ." Tell me, isn't she right?

But does he give a thought to his wife; does he give a thought to his children? Day in, day out, I have new worries with them—if it isn't one thing, it's another. As if all the trouble we had last year with the kopeck we thought Moishe-Hersheli swallowed wasn't enough—the other week he went and played a new trick (he's a devil, not a child!). He almost took himself off to the other world. He seemed quite sound and healthy, when suddenly I notice that the child isn't himself any longer—he keeps shaking his head and screams in a strange voice. "What's the matter with you, my sonny, my darling—tell me what's hurting you?" He points to his left ear with his little fingers and screams. I pummel and kiss him, I pinch and I hug him—but he doesn't stop screaming. On the third day I call the doctor. He asks me, that sage, if I looked into the child's ear. I tell him that not only did I look inside, but I even poked a knitting needle in it and couldn't find a thing! So he asks me what we ate last Sabbath. I answer: What does any Jew eat on Sabbath—radishes, onions, calf's-foot jelly, noodle pudding—anything else you want? Says he, "Maybe you cooked some beans or peas or such?" Say I, "And what if I did? If we did have some peas to eat, does that mean the child has to shake his head and scream?" Says he, "In all probability, if there were peas around the house, the child was playing with them; he may have poked one into his ear for fun, and now the pea has sprouted and swelled in his ear. . . ."

To make a long story short, he brought some kind of machine to the house; he tortured the poor child for half an hour and extracted a fistful of peas out of his ear! How do you like that? The whole world quietly gorges on peas and nothing happens! Miracles happen only to me. As Mother says, God bless her, "You have to be really unlucky to fall on a feather bed and crack your head. . . ."

That's why, my dearest husband, what good is your money-lending and all your affairs with Berdichev swindlers and defaulters? Better collect the few rubles you have and come home. Here you can also find work to do. As Mother says, God bless her, "One can get anything for money—except a fever . . ." which is the heartfelt wish of your really devoted wife,

Sheineh-Sheindl.

You know what favor I'll ask of you, Mendl? Please don't write me any more about your Yehupetz charlatans and their concubines—I don't even want to hear about such nasty things, may they roast alive! Better listen to what happened here: Levi-Moishe's precious son (they call him Borish after his grandfather Reb Berishl, that sot)—and a fine rascal he is, may he be the scapegoat for our little Moishe-Hersheli—well, the other day Borish and two beadles go to the shop of Liba, the wife of Moishe-Mordecai—and he says to Liba's daughter Feigele (Fanichka they call her these days!), "Fanichka, darling, please show me a finger!" So Fanichka shows him a finger. Then he takes a ring, puts it on her finger, and calls out to his two companions, "You are witnesses, gentlemen, that I have married her according to the Law of Moses and Israel!" You can imagine what a rumpus there was—plenty of noise and excitement. Liba promptly fainted away. The whole town came running to the shop to gloat over the show. Relatives butted in and ran off to ask the rabbi's advice. The rabbi says he has to give her a divorce. But Fanichka says she doesn't want a divorce! They have set their hearts on each other. It turns out this was planned by them long ago —what do you say to such impudence? Shouldn't all my troubles fall on her head?

7

Menahem-Mendl from Yehupetz to his wife,
Sheineh-Sheindl, in Kasrilevka

To my dear, wise, and modest helpmeet, Sheineh-Sheindl,
long may she live!

Firstly, I am come to inform you that I am, by the
grace of God, well and in good cheer. May the Lord,
blessed be His name, grant that we always hear from one
another none but the best, the most comforting, and the
happiest of tidings—amen.

And Secondly, I want you to know that money
business is suitable only for paupers. Moneylending may be
all very well, but the point is, it's only good if you have
money of your own. If you have to use somebody else's
money, it's a waste of time. You keep running around, and
it's all for nothing. God help you if you have to be at the
mercy of local moneylenders and usurers who sprout here
like nettles without benefit of rain. . . . And even the big
shots—the bankers, I mean—rather than crawl in front of
them, it's better to sit at home and cut coupons. . . .

In short, I have washed my hands of the moneylending
business and have started on houses. Why houses? Because
here, in Yehupetz, there's a new fad: houses! All the speculators have begun to deal in houses. You probably imagine
that in Yehupetz you buy a place to live in, the way you do
in Kasrilevka. Well, you're mistaken. When you buy a
house here in Yehupetz, you immediately carry it over to a

bank and get money for it; then you mortgage it and again get some money; then you rent the apartments and get some more money. In short, you buy a house without spending a single penny, and you become a houseowner painlessly. I suppose you'll ask, "In that case, can't everybody buy a house?" Well, there is one snag: Where to get money for the deposit? . . . But surely the good Lord will help me carry out the deal with which I am now playing around (I am just about to make a couple of houses). Then I'll buy a little house for myself (in your name) for about twenty thousand without investing a single red cent in it. Here is my calculation black on white: Fifteen thousand I get from the bank; six thousand I get on the second mortgage—well, doesn't that leave me with a thousand in cash in my pocket for expenses? What of the rental money and other blessings? How else do you think people get rich in Yehupetz? And since I'm busy and pressed for time, I must cut this short. Please God, in my next letter I'll write you everything in detail. For the time being, may the Lord grant health and success. Greet the children, God bless them, and give my kindest regards to everyone, to old and young, to big and small.

From me, your husband,
Menahem-Mendl.

Just remembered! Your story about the marriage in Liba's shop doesn't surprise me in the least. Here, in Yehupetz, having love affairs is very much in fashion. A young man and a young woman must, first of all, engage in a love affair; otherwise, the match won't be a success. Here, men very often throw their wives over and fall in love with other men's wives, or else the women throw their husbands over and fall in love with other women's husbands, and then the other man's wife falls in love with the other woman's husband's wife. . . . I mean, some other wife's husband. . . . Anyhow, in other words, they change around: What's mine is yours; what's yours is mine. . . . This isn't Kasrilevka—this is Yehupetz. . . .

         As above.

8

Sheineh-Sheindl from Kasrilevka to her husband, Menahem-Mendl, in Yehupetz

To my dear, esteemed, renowned, and honored husband, the wise and learned Menahem-Mendl, may his light shine forever.

I n t h e f i r s t p l a c e, I want to let you know that we are all, praise the Lord, perfectly well, and may we hear the same from you, please God, and never anything worse.

I n t h e s e c o n d p l a c e, I am writing to say, my dearest husband, I've never heard that a man can throw over his wife and children, his father-in-law and his mother-in-law, go off to a strange town and keep changing his business every day. Today he's making sugar, tomorrow he's a moneylender, and now he's suddenly building himself a house in Yehupetz without spending a single penny! Well, I guess it must be worthwhile! If I thought you were getting into debt over a house which is worth less than it costs you, I'd rather have it burn to an ash together with all the houses and palaces in Yehupetz. What a stroke of luck for me! After he pulls off a deal and makes a lot of money, he's going to buy me a house in my name! What do I need his houses for? Better send me some money, Mendl—I know what to buy with it myself. As Mother says, God bless her, "Just give me a loaf of bread—I can find a knife for it myself. . . ."

Somebody must have put a spell over me or else cast an

evil eye on me! If you ask me, I'm not any worse than Blumeh-Zlateh. I'm as good a Jewess as she, and as good-looking as she, and certainly as smart and as clever as she. So how have I deserved all this misery, God in heaven? Why have I got such terrible luck while every day Blumeh-Zlateh becomes broader than she is tall—may she get as thin as a stick! But come to think of it, what have I really got against Blumeh-Zlateh? She isn't trespassing on my property. May she be strong and healthy and live to a good old age with her Nehemia, and may the Lord help me in other ways. As Mother says, God bless her, "Don't look into other people's pots. . . ." It's just that it simply hurts me to see what a life others are leading—how they eat and how they dress, while I have to sit here like a live widow waiting for my wonderful breadwinner to get a stroke of luck, pick up what some beggar has dropped, and then build me a castle in Yehupetz! Yehupetz will never see the day I move there, renounce all my dear ones, throw my wig away, and become your concubine for the sake of your precious friends who swap wives—may they all lose their wigs together with their heads, which is the heartfelt wish of your really devoted wife,

Sheineh-Sheindl.

"One needn't have beauty," says my mother. "One needn't have brains—all one needs is luck." Take my Nehame-Braindl and Rachel, Aunt Dvora's daughter, for example. Nehame-Braindl is as beautiful as the summer sun; Rachel is as sour as vinegar. Nehame-Braindl, poor soul, is a spinster; Rachel is getting married. Her fiancé is a wretch from Yampol—actually, he's a fine, quiet, honest young man, only a bit of a booby. However, he comes from a very good family. They say he has a sister who became converted. The only flaw is that he isn't too strong—and yet for that very reason, he has nothing to fear from military conscription. It's a pleasure to look at that pair! She thinks there is no one smarter than he, and he thinks there is no one more beautiful than she. As Mother says, God bless her, "It is not beauty that one loves—what one loves is beautiful. . . ."

9

*Menahem-Mendl from Yehupetz to his wife,
Sheineh-Sheindl, in Kasrilevka*

To my dear, wise, and modest helpmeet, Sheineh-Sheindl,
long may she live!

F i r s t l y, I am come to inform you that I am, by the
grace of God, well and in good cheer. May the Lord, blessed
be His name, grant that we always hear from one another
none but the best, the most comforting, and the happiest
of tidings—amen.

A n d   S e c o n d l y, I want you to know, my dearest
wife, that the house business isn't worth a tinker's dam. I've
managed to wriggle out of it in the nick of time, and I've
started on a new line: estates. Dealing in estates is quite
a different kettle of fish. First of all, you save on shoe
leather. All you have to do is write a letter and send a "specification"; the buyer takes a trip, looks the land over, and,
please God, the deal is clinched. Second, you don't have
to have truck with a lot of paupers and swindlers. You deal
only with noblemen, squires, princes, and barons. You
probably ask how I come to barons; well, there's a long
tale attached to it.

As you already know, I am not allowed to live here. And
it often happens in the middle of the night that the police
make the rounds of lodging houses in order to see whether
everything is kosher. Usually, the landlady manages to
warn us in time so that we have a chance to melt away like

salt in water. One goes to Boiberik, another to Demievka, and the third to Slobodka. . . . But every once in a while the landlady herself doesn't know when the lightning will strike, and then God help us! Last week all of us lodgers were lying in bed fast asleep when we heard somebody knock. The landlady jumped out of bed trembling and shouted to us, "Jews, on your feet—beat a retreat!" We all rolled out of bed, and there was great rushing around and great excitement; some people hid in the cellar, but I went straight to my usual place in the attic, and right on my heels came another man, a Jew from Kaminetz. While I was cowering with fright, more dead than alive, I hear the poor fellow sigh. "What are you sighing for?" I whisper to him. "Ah, me," he says, "I've left all my papers under my pillow. I'm afraid for my papers!" "What kind of papers?" I ask. "Ah, me," he says, "very important papers! I don't exaggerate—they're worth maybe half a million!" When I heard "half a million," I quietly moved closer to the fellow and asked: "How come you have so many papers, and what are they all about?" "It's estates," he says. "I've got estates in the Vohlin District—wonderful huge estates, completely stocked with horses and oxen and no end of sheep—with water mills, distilleries, large yards, excellent gardens and orchards, everything of the finest!" When I heard this, I edged still closer to my neighbor. "How come you have so many estates with all those wonderful treasures?" "The estates," he tells me, "do not grow in my backyard. They belong to noblemen, and they fell into my lap. That is, I am their agent, and that's the reason I've come here and brought all the papers and specifications. What do you think—will any harm come to them, God forbid?" "Perish the thought!" I say. "Who's going to touch another man's property? Only may the Almighty watch over us and

keep us from being found in this attic." And in the meantime, I start pumping him, "Well, have you done anything
about your estates as yet?" "No," says he, "nothing at all
for the time being. I'm afraid of the local brokers," he says.
"They are all terrible liars. You'll never hear a word of
truth from them. Maybe you happen to know an estate
broker? Only he's got to be a *real* broker, and above all an
honest man who doesn't tell lies!" "Oh," I say, "by
all means! Myself! I am an estate broker," I say. "That is to
say, so far I have never handled any estates in my life, but
never mind!" I say. "If the good Lord were to send me a
buyer, I'd know how to deal with estates, too." "I see," he
says, "that I am talking to a really honest man. So give me
your hand and your word of honor that this will remain between us, and I'll hand all the papers over to you and tell
you all the particulars." To make a long story short, we made
a deal. That is to say, we decided to go into partnership on
every deal. He is investing all his estates in the partnership, and I am investing my buyers. And since I am busy
and pressed for time, I must cut this short. Please God, in
my next letter I'll write you everything in detail. For the
time being, may the Lord grant health and success. Greet
the children, God bless them, and give my kindest regards
to everyone, to old and young, to big and small.

From me, your husband,
Menahem-Mendl.

Just remembered! The panic at the lodging
house turned out to be a false alarm. It was simply a neighbor knocking at our windows by mistake, so we hid away
all for nothing! But this only goes to show the wonderful
ways of God. If, for instance, that neighbor had not knocked
on the window, there wouldn't have been an alarm. Then

I wouldn't have gone to the attic, and I wouldn't have met the man from Kaminetz, and I wouldn't have learned anything about estates and barons. Now all I need is a bit of luck!

As above.   ·

10

Sheineh-Sheindl from Kasrilevka to her husband, Menahem-Mendl, in Yehupetz

To my dear, esteemed, renowned, and honored husband, the wise and learned Menahem-Mendl, may his light shine forever.

In the first place, I want to let you know that we are all, praise the Lord, perfectly well, and may we hear the same from you, please God, and never anything worse.

In the second place, I am writing to say that I caught a very bad cold, may all your concubines in Yehupetz catch it from me. I am coughing, and I'm drinking goat's milk, and I've also been to see the doctor. During the past years the doctors have squeezed plenty of money out of me, may they choke on it together with the druggists! The only stroke of luck is that a new druggist's shop has recently opened in town, and now one can bargain with the druggists.

Congratulations on your new business—the estates and the barons! Isn't it wonderful the way he throws businesses around, a new one every day! Besides being such a roaring success, he has to be choosy in the bargain, and he finds fault with every new business he undertakes. As Mother says, God bless her, "When a girl doesn't know how to dance, she blames it on the fiddler. . . ."

I'm very much afraid, Mendl, that after trying your hand at every possible business, you'll end by peddling matches

—like Getzl, Aunt Sossi's son, who went to America expecting to find a crock of gold, and now he writes letters that could melt even a stone. He writes that over there, in America, everybody has to work by the sweat of his brow; otherwise, your belly swells with hunger, and nobody offers you even a piece of bread. What a wonderful country —may it burn to an ash along with your Yehupetz! But that's exactly what all of you deserve. As Mother says, God bless her, "If you've got a piece of bread, take your eyes off the cake. . . ." God grant I never get such news of you as comes from Getzl—or maybe even far worse, which is the heartfelt wish of your devoted wife,

Sheineh-Sheindl.

Mother says, God bless her, "Thieves and rogues have the best of luck if they only escape hanging! . . ." A government official has arrived here. He has been sticking his nose into every hole and cranny, sniffing and smelling and eavesdropping in order to find out what happened to the money which Moishe-Mordecai left to charity. Some rascals have informed him that the money has remained in the pocket of our Mr. Rich Man, but the latter has produced an accounting to show that it was all properly distributed, and now it's gone! Where has it gone to? It's gone with the wind and the smoke. . . . May he go along with it to Siberia, in fetters. . . .

I I

Menahem-Mendl from Yehupetz to his wife,
Sheineh-Sheindl, in Kasrilevka

To my dear, wise, and modest helpmeet, Sheineh-Sheindl,
long may she live!

F i r s t l y, I am come to inform you that I am, by the
grace of God, well and in good cheer. May the Lord, blessed
be His name, grant that we always hear from one another
none but the best, the most comforting, and the happiest
of tidings—amen.

A n d S e c o n d l y, I want you to know, my dearest
wife, that already I have more than a million rubles' worth
of estates. I have amazing bargains—wonders of the world!
You'll probably ask how all these treasures came to me, so
just listen to this.

When I appeared on the exchange together with my Kaminetz partner and let it be understood that I have estates
for sale, we were immediately besieged by a mob of brokers who also have estates for sale. So we all made a deal:
We swapped estate for estate. That is to say, we gave them
the specifications of our estates, and they gave us the specifications of *theirs*. Just figure it out: If *we* manage to sell
their estates, we'll certainly make money. If they manage
to sell *our* estates, we'll again be making money. Whatever
the case, we shall certainly lose nothing!

In short, I've managed to break into the brokers' circle,
and, thank God, I am now enjoying a broker's standing
among the biggest of them. I can already sit at a marble-

topped table in Semedeni's Cafe like the best of them—
just as in Odessa—and I drink coffee and eat butter cakes,
which is the custom here; otherwise, a man comes and
chases you out. The real market is at Semedeni's. All the
brokers of the world gather here. There is always noise
here, and an uproar and disorder—just like in a synagogue,
may I be forgiven the comparison. Everybody is talking,
laughing, and sawing the air with their hands. Sometimes a
quarrel breaks out and words are exchanged, and then it
gets patched up, because whenever there is a commission
to be divided, there is always room for argument, for curses,
insults, thumbing of noses, slaps, and me in the middle.
And since I am very busy and pressed for time, I must cut
this short. Please God, in my next letter I'll write you everything in detail. For the time being, may the Lord grant
health and success. Greet the children, God bless them, and
give my kindest regards to your father and mother, to old
and young, to big and small.

From me, your husband,
Menahem-Mendl.

Just remembered! One of my estates in the Vohlin District has a palace standing on it. It has sixty-six
rooms. The walls, the ceilings, and the floors are all made of
mirror glass. And there's a garden called a hothouse where
oranges and lemons grow summer and winter. And all the
horses and carriages simply knock your eye out—and all
of this is on sale at half price! If the Lord were to send me a
good buyer, would there be anyone to match me? There's
only one little snag: Most real estate brokers are long in
the tongue—that is to say, they sometimes like to exaggerate the quality of their merchandise. But what can one
do? For the sake of business, sometimes one is even forced
to lie. . . .

As above.

12

Sheineh-Sheindl from Kasrilevka to her husband, Menahem-Mendl, in Yehupetz

To my dear, esteemed, renowned, and honored husband, the wise and learned Menahem-Mendl, may his light shine forever.

In the first place, I want to let you know that we are all, praise the Lord, perfectly well, and may we hear the same from you, please God, and never anything worse.

In the second place, I am writing to say, my dearest husband, that I have started to spit blood because of your wonderful letters. I am ashamed to show anybody what you write to me. As Mother says, God bless her, "The worst pain is the one you have to hide. . . ." Will you please explain to me what is the sense of spending the whole day drinking coffee and eating butter cakes in the middle of the week at Sima-Dina's (who in the world is she? In our town there used to be a midwife called Sima-Dina, but she passed away long ago). Just fancy, he's got estates for sale! A Garden of Eden with sixty-six rooms— sixty-six plagues on the heads of my enemies! Because, after all, what does it matter to him, over there in Yehupetz, that I have to worry myself sick over his children? Yesterday, for instance, my little Lea, God bless her, quarreled with Moishe-Hersheli, may he live to be a hundred, and she whacked him in the face with a fork and only by luck missed his eye!

But what's the use of talking when it goes into one ear and out of the other? It's plain murder! I write letter after letter—I simply burst with aggravation—and he sits pretty in Yehupetz, drinking coffee, eating butter cakes, and watching brokers pummel one another on the market! If the good Lord were only to send one of those brokers to square accounts with you and give you a bit of what you deserve, then maybe he'd beat some sense into your head, which is the heartfelt wish of your really devoted wife,

Sheineh-Sheindl.

You can be proud of your "aristocrats," Mendl, shame on them! You ought to see what's going on in town with our two young doctors—Dr. Clove and Dr. Licorice. They're fighting like two tomcats. Dr. Clove took the trouble to inform on Dr. Licorice that he had—no more, no less—poisoned a child. . . . So Dr. Licorice goes and informs on Dr. Clove that working hand in hand with Feivl, the insurance agent, he insured a corpse in the Anchor Company. . . . So Dr. Clove went and informed on Dr. Licorice. . . . But may both of them answer for my sins, for the sins of my whole family, all my dear ones, and all of Israel, amen!

13

*Menahem-Mendl from Yehupetz to his wife,
Sheineh-Sheindl, in Kasrilevka*

To my dear, wise, and modest helpmeet, Sheineh-Sheindl,
long may she live!

F i r s t l y, I am come to inform you that I am, by the
grace of God, well and in good cheer. May the Lord,
blessed be His name, grant that we always hear from one
another none but the best, the most comforting, and the
happiest of tidings—amen.

A n d S e c o n d l y, I want you to know that now I am
dealing only in forests, because an estate without a forest
is like a house without a chimney. The crown, the jewel, of
an estate is the forest. Forests have feathered the nest of
many a Jew—they have made millions! But you'll probably
ask how I ever got to a forest. Well, you'll see how the Almighty arranges things.

When I became an estate broker and started hanging
around other brokers, I happened to meet one of the big
shots. He asks me, "What have you got? Show me your merchandise!" So I take out my parcel of estate inventories,
totaling a million and seven hundred thousand shekels. He
takes one look at them and says, "I hope you don't mind my
saying so, but all your estates aren't worth three pinches of
snuff." So I ask him, "Why so?" Says he to me, "Because
everyone of your estates is stark naked—they have nothing
but land and sky, sky and land. Where are the forests?

What good is an estate to me if it hasn't got a forest? . . .
Why don't you say something? I want a forest! Give me a
forest!" I confess I held my tongue because I was absolutely
overcome with shame at the idea that I've been peddling
merchandise which can't even be called merchandise! "If
that is a fact," I say to him, "why don't you let me have a
real piece of real estate, including a forest? I have some
buyers." "Oh," says he, "with pleasure! I have," says he,
"a wonderful forest for you—the foot of man has never yet
trodden in it. It has trees," he says, "which started growing
on the first day of creation—oaks as high as the firmament,
cedars of Lebanon. On one side there's a railroad, on the
other a river. And where do you think that river is?" says
he. "Look—here is the forest, and there is the river. Chop
down a tree, and—splash!—right into the water! . . ."
When I heard this, I immediately ran off to scare up a
buyer for this forest, and the Lord was good to me. I managed to snap one up. I tracked him down through a broker,
naturally, and *that* broker found him through another
broker. But that doesn't matter. If the business works out,
God willing, there will be enough profit to go around.

When I finally reached the buyer myself and told him I
have a forest from the Year One, with a railroad on one
side, a river on the other, chop down a tree, and—splash!
—right into the water, the proposition seemed to appeal
to him at once. So he put me on the carpet and quizzed me
in the science of forestry: What is the name of the forest,
where is it located, what kinds of trees grow there, how tall
are they, how wide are their trunks, where do the branches
start growing, what kind of bark have they got, what are the
rings like, how does one get to the place, what is the road
like, and is there lots of snow in the winter. . . . In short,
he simply deluged me with questions and didn't give me a
chance to open my mouth. When he reached the bottom of

his lungs, he finally said, "Why waste words? Bring me an inventory of the forest, and then we'll start talking. . . ."

"What do you need an inventory for?" I say. "All I have to do is take a single leap and I'll bring you the seller himself—the owner of the forest—that's better than any inventory!"

To make a long story short, I ran off to look for my seller, nabbed him, and brought him straight to the buyer's hotel room. The moment my buyer and my seller laid eyes on each other, they burst out laughing so hard I thought they'd both get a stroke. "So this is the owner of your forest!" says the buyer. "So this is the buyer of your forest!" says the seller. The door opens, and in come two other men, and without wasting a single word, they open up a card table, bring out the cards, we all sit down to play Hearts, and business is postponed for the next day, God willing, and since I am very busy and pressed for time, I must cut this short. Please God, in my next letter, I'll write you everything in detail. For the time being, may the Lord grant health and success. Greet the children, God bless them, and give my kindest regards to your father and mother, to old and young, to big and small.

> From me, your husband,
> Menahem-Mendl.

14

Sheineh-Sheindl from Kasrilevka to her husband, Menahem-Mendl, in Yehupetz

To my dear, esteemed, renowned, and honored husband, the wise and learned Menahem-Mendl, may his light shine forever.

In the first place, I want to let you know that we are all, praise the Lord, perfectly well, and may we hear the same from you, please God, and never anything worse.

In the second place, I am writing to say, my dearest husband, that my life cannot be called life at all. As Mother says, God bless her, "If that's the way you have to ride, better go on foot. . . ." I can just imagine, woe is me! what your merchants are like if, when they get together to discuss a million-ruble forest deal, they drop everything, lock, stock, and barrel, and sit down to play Hearts throuoghout the night! . . . They should have the kind of pain in their hearts that I have in my chest! . . . Unhappy me, what did I do to deserve such a bitter fate— my husband, who never knew a card from a shard, is now busy writing me about card games! Have you nothing better to do, Mendl, than turn gambler in your old age and put your family to shame? And then those forests! What have you got to do with forests? Have you ever seen a tree grow? As Mother says, God bless her, "What business has a rabbi in a pigsty? . . ." I am afraid your forests will end just like all your other golden affairs which start with fortune and end in misfortune, which is the heartfelt wish of your really devoted wife,

Sheineh-Sheindl.

The whole world is talking about you, Mendl! The other day, your relative Kreindl, may she answer for my sins, met me and my mother in the market at the fishmonger's and started lamenting and weeping over me! May she herself be lamented soon! Why don't I, says she, put an end to all this business and get a divorce from you? . . . You can imagine, Mother didn't let her get away with it. Don't for a moment think that Mother, God forbid, quarreled with her or scolded her. She simply let go with some of her sayings, as only she knows how: "When two cats are aspitting, the third should be aflitting. . . . An old pot is better than a new shard. . . . Good friends are like nettles— they grow without benefit of rain. . . . If you have a rope, why not hang yourself first? . . . Look at the beam in your own eye. . . . If you eat garlic, you can't smell the onion on your neighbor's breath. . . . Though the ox has a long tongue, it can't blow its horn . . ." and a whole string of similar sayings, God bless Mother, till Kreindl finally took to her heels as she completely lost the use of her tongue.

15

Menahem-Mendl from Yehupetz to his wife,
Sheineh-Sheindl, in Kasrilevka

To my dear, wise, and modest helpmeet, Sheineh-Sheindl,
long may she live!

F i r s t l y , I am come to inform you that I am, by the
grace of God, well and in good cheer. May the Lord,
blessed be His name, grant that we always hear from one
another none but the best, the most comforting, and the
happiest of tidings—amen.

A n d S e c o n d'l y , I want you to know, my dearest
wife, that the forest has turned out to be a treeless valley.
There is no forest—there is not even a bear cub in sight.
No trees, no river, nothing but clouds and wind, a pipe
dream, a pot of gold at the end of the rainbow, last year's
snow! I have led others and myself by the nose, all
for nothing! Walked my legs off, wore my shoes out—all
for nothing!

I now see, my dearest wife, that forests are not for me,
and doing business with such liars is also beyond me. They
can talk you into seeing a cow jump over the moon, and
thanks to them, you find yourself six feet underground!
So what did I do? In the nick of time I switched to another business: refineries. (That's what sugar factories are
called.) Today it's the best business of all. Jews are buying
up refineries, and brokers are making money on them—
amassing fortunes! There's a broker here who managed to

wangle his way among the Radomysl sugar people; every
day he sells two or three refineries, pockets ten to fifteen
thousand in commissions, and goes home for the Sabbath!
What more do you want? Even servants and agents have
become refinery experts; they wear golden watches, they
talk German, they have even begun to suffer from ulcers,
and they send their wives to watering resorts—that's how
terribly aristocratic they've become! In a word, there is
only one business left on the Yehupetz exchange—refineries! All the brokers are now making refineries, and me
in the middle. But you probably want to know how I've
managed to worm my way into such a substantial business,
considering that I don't even know whether one has to use
a fork or a spoon for it. Wait and you'll hear about God's
ways with man.

Some time ago, I stopped going to Semedeni's (not
Sima-Dina, as you call him—it's actually a man, not a
woman, and a nasty piece of goods in the bargain), and I
stopped going there not because I quarreled with him, but
simply because I got sick and tired of coffee and rolls, and
as a matter of fact, my pocket was quite empty—so I started
ambling about the streets, like all the other Jews. I ambled
and ambled until I met a refinery broker, who struck me as
a very honest man with big connections. According to him,
he has access to the biggest offices, even Brodsky's. So he
says to me, "Where does a Jew hail from?" "From Kasrilevka," I tell him. "As a matter of fact," I say, "Yampol
is where I really come from; Mazepovka is where I am
registered as a resident; Kasrilevka is where my family
lives, and, as for me, I am doing business in Yehupetz."
"And what exactly is Kasrilevka," he asks, "a village or a
townlet?" "What do you mean, a townlet?" I say. "It's a
whole town!" "Are Jews permitted to live there?" he asks.
"I should say so!" I reply. "Is that a fact?" says he. "Maybe

you've got a river there?" "And what a river!" I say. "It's called Stinko River." "Is that a fact?" says he. "And what about a railway—is it far away?" "Only some fifty miles," I say. "But why are you asking all those questions?" "Give me your hand," he says, "and swear this will remain between us. I have a piece of good news for you, Reb Menahem-Mendl: Very, very soon, please God, we are going to earn money, and lots of it—enough to fill your cap! This very moment an idea has struck me—it's the sort of idea one gets once in a hundred years. And it is this: These days, there are lots of refinery buyers around—but refineries are hard to come by. All available refineries have already been purchased by Radomysl people, and there aren't any more for sale. Therefore, people have started building brand-new refineries, as fresh as a fresh carp, and since Jews are not allowed in villages, one can look for refinery sites only in those little towns where Jews are permitted to live. Now do you see that it was written in the books that your Kasrilevka should be a site for a refinery? Take a good look at me—I happen to have a client who'll invest half a million in building a refinery, but I haven't got any site for it. All available places have already been snatched up. Maybe you know," he says, "whom to talk to in Kasrilevka and whether there are any beets there and an empty plot on which to build a refinery?" "Oh," say I, "by all means! I have there," say I, "a wife till a hundred and twenty years, also a father- and mother-in-law and a whole gaggle of relatives. I can write them immediately, and you can rest assured," I say, "that I'll get a reply describing everything from Dan to Beersheba, by return of mail!" And that's why, my dearest wife, I am writing you about this, and I ask you to go see Azriel, the village elder, and Red Moshke, the fellow who tags after noblemen, and tell him to feel them out about an available plot, and how many beets one can have, and what the price is, and immediately send me a letter because, you understand, this is very important and we could make a nice fat pile of almost ten or fifteen thousand! And since I am very busy and pressed for time, I must cut this short. Please God, in my next letter, I shall write you everything in detail. For the time being, may the Lord grant health and success. Greet the children, God bless them, and give my kindest regards to everyone, to old and young, to big and small.

From me, your husband,
Menahem-Mendl.

J u s t   r e m e m b e r e d! I asked my present partner who his buyer is, and I learned that his buyer is also from Radomysl—and a very hot buyer, too (since all Radomysl people are very hot buyers—they simply burn to buy refineries, even if it's only a windmill, as long as there's a chimney on top of it, and it whistles). I therefore hope to heaven that this business materializes, please God, and then we'll certainly make money, with the Lord's help, even though quite a number of partners are involved in this deal. I'm afraid they add up to a whole minyan—ten souls! But never mind, so long as the business turns out to be, God willing, a real deal; as you know, I'm in no hurry to get rich!

As above.

16

Sheineh-Sheindl from Kasrilevka to her husband, Menahem-Mendl, in Yehupetz

To my dear, esteemed, renowned, and honored husband, the wise and learned Menahem-Mendl, may his light shine forever.

In the first place, I want to let you know that we are all, praise the Lord, perfectly well, and may we hear the same from you, please God, and never anything worse.

In the second place, I am writing to say that I've read and reread your scroll, and I didn't understand a single word of it! You ask whether there are any free plots in Kasrilevka. I can tell you there are plenty of free plots in the new cemetery—enough to supply all your partners, with half the population of Yehupetz thrown in! And why do you keep harping on beets? Why don't you ask also about cabbages and turnips or horseradish? And our river! Have you forgotten what our river is like? May your partners' tongues be as dry as its riverbed! Come Passover, one drinks water with frogs, and during the summer the river gets choked with green weeds. I'd like to see your fine Yehupetz friends, who suffer with their digestions, come and drink our water during the summer months. . . . No, Mendl, let them remain in Yehupetz with their stomach-aches—we'll manage to get along without their refineries. As my mother says, God bless her, "What's a cockroach to a cock? . . ." Knock all that nonsense out of your silly head.

You'll sell refineries exactly the way you've sold forests, estates, houses, and sugar! Rest assured that before you have time to look around, your partners will swindle you from head to foot, because you've always been a ne'er-do-well and will remain a ne'er-do-well, which is the heartfelt wish of your really devoted wife,

Sheineh-Sheindl.

Oh, yes, please tell me, Mendl, what's this we've been hearing? They say that in Yehupetz people are getting registered for the Holy Land. Anybody who pays a deposit of forty kopecks will go to the Holy Land. What is it all about? The whole town is talking about it. The young people gather every night at the home of Yossl, Moishe-Yossi's son-in-law, just to talk about the Holy Land. In a word, there's quite a stew about it. As Mother says, God bless her, "It's been too peaceful to last. . . ."

17

*Menahem-Mendl from Yehupetz to his wife,
Sheineh-Sheindl, in Kasrilevka*

To my dear, wise, and modest helpmeet, Sheineh-Sheindl,
long may she live!

F i r s t l y, I am come to inform you that I am, by the
grace of God, well and in good cheer. May the Lord,
blessed be His name, grant that we always hear from one
another none but the best, the most comforting, and the
happiest of tidings—amen.

A n d S e c o n d l y, I want you to know, my dearest wife,
that the refinery business has cooled off considerably. It
has suffered a crisis. Refineries are now practically clutter-
ing up the streets—there are no takers! You see, the world
has overgorged itself on refineries and overshot the mark;
money is dear, and sugar is cheap as dirt. Because such a
lot of sugar was produced, there's nothing to do but chuck
it out! The business has bit the dust. Manufacturers are
pining away for a penny, capitalists are holding back, and
brokers are out of a job, with not a thing to do, and me in
the middle.

You probably think it's the end of the world? Oh, no,
you are not to worry, my dearest wife. God is eternal, and
Yehupetz is still a city. People like me don't go under,
heaven forbid. On the contrary, only now do I feel confident that, God willing, I am bound to rise in the world
because I am now working on a deal which must bring, as

my share, almost one hundred thousand rubles! The business which I am handling is worth ten million, and maybe even more than ten—in fact, there's no limit to it and no value on it! It stands to reason that there must be thousands of rubles worth of gold alone, over there. And what about the silver, and the iron, and the copper, and the tin, and the quicksilver? I'm not even going to mention the coal and the granite! Besides, you've got forests there, too, and fields and anything else your heart desires. They say it is an absolute gold mine, and all they ask for it is two and a half million. It's a bargain even for a thief! There is only one drawback—it's a bit too far—in fact, it is stuck away somewhere in Siberia, and it takes all of three weeks maybe to get there, because no railway goes so far.

To whom can one offer such a big deal? Brodsky, naturally! So there is another snag: How does one break into Brodsky's office? First of all, in front of the door stands a doorman with bright buttons who looks you all over to see how you're dressed—a shabby coat is given no entrance. And then if, God willing, you do manage to bypass the doorman, you have to wait about six hours on the staircase before the Lord takes pity on you and you are granted a glimpse of Brodsky passing by. And if you have the good luck to lay your eyes on him, the chances are that he whizzes past you like an arrow, and before you have time to turn around, he is already sitting in his carriage and— hail and farewell! So you have to be polite enough to return the next day. The next day the show starts all over again—and no wonder, considering how many affairs he has to deal with! So it isn't very easy to get to him, but I haven't lost hope someday to break through, and then we can get down to business. And since I'm so busy and pressed for time, I must cut this short. Please God, in my next letter, I'll write you everything in detail. For the time being, may the Lord grant health and success. Greet the children, God bless them, and give my kindest regards to everyone, to old and young, to big and small.

From me, your husband,
Menahem-Mendl.

Just remembered! As for your question about the Holy Land, I suppose you're talking about Zionism. This is a very noble idea, even though they don't seem to think much of it on the Yehupetz exchange. I have attended several Zionist meetings because I wanted to find out what it's all about. But they all talked Russian—and even that, at great length. Seems to me, it wouldn't hurt anybody if Jews talked Yiddish to one another. . . . Several times I even tried to discuss it with my companions on the exchange, but they only made fun of me: "Stuff and nonsense! Zionism! Dr. Herzl! Is that a deal, too?"

As above.

18

Sheineh-Sheindl from Kasrilevka to her husband, Menahem-Mendl, in Yehupetz

To my dear, esteemed, renowned, and honored husband, the wise and learned Menahem-Mendl, may his light shine forever.

In the first place, I want to let you know that we are all, praise the Lord, perfectly well, and may we hear the same from you, please God, and never anything worse.

In the second place, I am writing to say, my dearest husband, that my Gittl lost her husband and was left with seven little orphans, one smaller than the next. My brother-in-law, may he rest in peace, died of a toothache. That is to say, strictly speaking, he never was very strong. In fact, he used to spit quite a lot of blood, may I be spared his fate. Nevertheless, we all thought he'd manage to last for some time. Finally, he goes and has a tooth pulled by Shmelke, the doctor; then he returns home, lies down, and dies. As Mother says, long may she live, "Nobody knows when his tomorrow is due. . . ."

In the meantime, poor Gittl is rending the skies with her wails; her grief is not to be described. I suppose if, perish the thought, it were the other way around and my sister, long may she live, were to die, God forbid, and Zalman-Meir were to be widowed, he certainly would not shed so many tears. In all probability, right after the thirty days of mourning, he'd go to Berdichev and bring a step-mother for his children. I'm saying this about husbands in general, may they all answer for their wives' sins. Because it is absolutely unheard of that a father of children should get a flea in his ear—millions! How fortunate he is—he is allowed to stand in front of Brodsky's door! I'm afraid you'll never get much farther than that door. Save your shoe leather! Do you expect Brodsky to pull his millions out of his purse at once and fly to Siberia? And why? Because Menahem-Mendl heard with his own ears somewhere, the devil knows where, that gold and quicksilver are rolling on the ground! As Mother says, God bless her, "A deaf man heard a mute man say that a blind man saw a lame man run. . . ."

Don't I know in advance that in your next letter you are sure to write that the gold mine has turned to ashes? But of course, soon again you'll find another swindler with a new dream who will tell you that a cow flew over the roof and laid an egg, and you'll pick up your coattails and again start running around like mad. You might, however, stop to think that at home you have a wife till a hundred and twenty years and little children who are longing to see you—maybe this will stop you from going from door to door and occupying yourself with rubbish which is enough to make anyone's gall rise! But I see you have not learned sense in Yehupetz, may it burn to an ash, which is the heartfelt wish of your really devoted wife,

Sheineh-Sheindl.

Here is a nice story for you, though a short one. You remember Meir, Meshulam's son? Well, Meir has a daughter called Shprinzl. She was a healthy girl, strong as iron—maybe a little overripe, but quite diligent. Well, a bookseller came peddling storybooks from house to house and lending out novels. So poor Shprinzl pounced on those storybooks and novels as if they were something really worthwhile, and they say she gobbled up maybe a hundred books. And from that moment on, it seems she got mixed up in her head, may I be spared the same. She now talks in a funny way and keeps saying things nobody can understand. She says her name isn't Shprinzl. It's "Bertha." And any minute she keeps expecting somebody called Lord, her "protector"; he is going to sneak into her room through the window and take her the devil knows where—to London, I think, and from London to Stambul—may they burst, all those empty-headed inventors of drivel and fiddle-daddle!

19

Menahem-Mendl from Yehupetz to his wife,
Sheineh-Sheindl, in Kasrilevka

To my dear, wise, and modest helpmeet, Sheineh-Sheindl,
long may she live!

F i r s t l y, I am come to inform you that I am, by the
grace of God, well and in good cheer. May the Lord,
blessed be His name, grant that we always hear from one
another none but the best, the most comforting, and the
happiest of tidings—amen.

A n d S e c o n d l y, I want you to know, my dearest
wife, that our Lord is great. Just listen to this. Ever since
I started visiting at Brodsky's, I've become a general favorite on the exchange, and brokers are streaming to me from
every corner of the earth with thousands of propositions:
houses and estates, forests and railways, steamships and
factories—all worth millions—and everything, mind you,
thanks to Brodsky. Among all those brokers, there are two
partners, neither from this part of the country. One of
them wears a peculiar cape (it is called an inverness), and
the other has such an odd name that I'm ashamed to put it
down on paper. . . . One day, as I was coming from
Brodsky's, these two brokers nabbed me, and the Cape
addressed me as follows: "Listen to what we have to say to
you, Mr. Menaham-Mendl. This is our story: We've heard
that you hang around Brodsky's. Well, may God add
strength to you, we have nothing against that." "In that

event," say I, "what do you want?" "What do we want?" he
repeats. "All we want is what every broker wants. We want
to earn money. We are also brokers. We also have propositions, and who knows, with a little effort on your part and
a little on our own, maybe we can make a deal and divide
the profits. That way there may be less to earn, but at least
we'll earn something. How does the saying go? 'Three heads
are better than one'. . ." "In any event," say I, "why
waste time on long speeches? Better tell me what you have.
Don't be shy." "We have," says he, "very, very many propositions, with God's grace. We have coal in the Poltava
District; we have iron in Kanyev County; we have a
burned-down mill in Pereyaslav; we have brand-new
machines invented by a Jew in Pinsk; there is also a nobleman who wants to swap a forest for a distillery; and we
have a man who wants to buy a large house in Yehupetz
without money. As for estates! Or forests! If you have any
buyers, we'll give you the estates, and if you have any estates, we'll give you the buyers." "Oh, no," say I, "I don't
deal in estates and forests any longer—that's finished! I
got scorched on estates and on forests," I say, "and I swore
not to touch a single forest or an estate with my littlest
finger!" "Ah," says the Cape, "but are all propositions
alike? For example, we now have an estate with oil—in
the Caucasus—that is to say there is soil on it which squirts
oil. It squirts and squirts and doesn't stop squirting. There
is not a shadow of a doubt that the soil can spit out a million tons of oil in a single day! . . ." "In that event," I say,
"you are just the people for me. That's what I call a deal!"
I say. "Such a deal you can hand over to me at once!"

So the three of us went off to the Jewish Dairy. (I
stopped going to Semedeni's because they throw people
out of there, so now I patronize the Jewish Dairy—it's
cozier to be among a Jewish crowd, and you can spend a

whole day talking and doing whatever you wish.) There we discussed the deal thoroughly and entered into a partnership. When it came to signing the contract, they let the cat out of the bag: Several other partners were involved in this deal—there is a man with thick lips; another is a redhead who deals in watches (and can spin a long yarn!) ; a third one has a raspberry nose, with red blotches on it, and is also quite an expert at exaggerating; and even a fourth one who is a widower. When I heard how many partners there were, I got cold feet. However, the Cape talked such a lot around and about me and so persuasively that finally I had to agree to sign the paper. It goes without saying that there must always be some disagreement among partners: Everybody thinks he deserves the bigger share. But if the Almighty were only to help me finish with the second party to this deal as easily as I finished with the brokers, it won't be too bad because how can anybody earn less than a million on such a deal, God willing? And so I promised myself that if the deal comes through, please God, I shall immediately rent a small office on Nikolayevsky Street and become a big broker, by the grace of the Lord. And since I am very busy and pressed for time, I must cut this short. Please God, in my next letter I'll write you everything in detail. For the time being, may the Lord grant health and success. Greet the children, God bless them, and give my kindest regards to everyone, to old and young, to big and small.

From me, your husband,
Menahem-Mendl.

Just remembered! There was something very important I wanted to tell you, but I forget what it is. So, God willing, I'll leave it for the next time.

As above.

20

Sheineh-Sheindl from Kasrilevka to her husband, Menahem-Mendl, in Yehupetz

To my dear, esteemed, renowned, and honored husband, the wise and learned Menahem-Mendl, may his light shine forever.

In the first place, I want to let you know that we are all, praise the Lord, perfectly well, and may we hear the same from you, please God, and never anything worse.

In the second place, I am writing to say, my dearest husband, that I am not writing much because I have no strength left to write and to give you a piece of my mind. It is like beating one's head against the wall. As Mother says, God bless her, "You can play a sad tune for the bridegroom, but it won't alter his thoughts. . . ." Maybe you are a general favorite in Yehupetz because you are spending your days on Brodsky's doorstep and scattering millions around—that still doesn't mean you have the right to be high and mighty. Because the millions are still in Brodsky's pocket and not in yours, and it may very well turn out that the earth which is supposed to squirt olive oil will squirt nothing but soda water, and the whole marvelous deal will end in blows—and who'll be on the receiving end? Yourself! So my advice to you is to wriggle out of it in time and return home. You must forget about the past—maybe I've offended you with a harsh word once upon a time. As Mother says, God bless her, "Better a blow from a friend than a kiss from an enemy. . . ." So please dash a telegram off to me, come home as soon as possible, and put an end to all this, which is the heartfelt wish of your really devoted wife,

Sheineh-Sheindl.

I have to tell you about something that happened here and set the whole town agog. You remember Meir-Mottl, the son-in-law of Moishe-Meir? Well, Meir-Mottl has a daughter, Rachel. This Rachel is something special invented by the Almighty. She is still a "mademoiselle," trained and groomed in all the arts: she twitters in French, pounds on the piano, and keeps herself to herself. And no wonder if you just think of her family tree: Her grandfather was a butcher! As Mother says, God bless her, "A skeleton in the cupboard is better than dust. . . ."

To make a long story short, she's had her pick of all kinds of suitors from all corners of the earth, but she is very choosy: No candidate you offer is good enough for her. She wants a husband with every imaginable virtue: He must be handsome and clever and rich—in short, an angel from the sky. All the matchmakers have worn themselves to the bone. Finally, they found a paragon of all virtues—a gem, a bargain, a treasure, and—would you believe it!—from a small town (called Avrutch)! After the fiancé was brought for inspection, the young couple was left alone in a room as usual in order to give them a chance to look each other over. Says the bride to the fiancé, "What are they saying about Dreyfus in your town?" Says he, "Which Dreyfus?" Says she to him, "You don't know which Dreyfus?" Says he, "No, what does he deal in? . . ." So she bursts out of the room and faints, and the poor fiancé has to return to his town in disgrace. That's the end of him; that's the end of her; that's the end of both of them!

And by the way, since you are among people of the world, will you please explain to me who is this Dreyfus, and why is the whole world making such a fuss over him?

21

Menahem-Mendl from Yehupetz to his wife,
Sheineh-Sheindl, in Kasrilevka

To my dear, wise, and modest helpmeet, Sheineh-Sheindl,
long may she live!

F i r s t l y, I am come to inform you that I am, by the
grace of God, well and in good cheer. May the Lord,
blessed be His name, grant that we always hear from one
another none but the best, the most comforting, and the
happiest of tidings—amen.

A n d S e c o n d l y, I want you to know, my dearest
wife, that I have broken off with Brodsky. Not that we've
quarreled, God forbid. I simply stopped going there.
What do I need Brodsky for, when I'm about to do business with Rothschild in Paris?! You probably want to
know how I, Menahem-Mendl, got to Rothschild in Paris?
Well, it's the same old story: Caucasus and oil all over
again. All these oils in the Caucasus belong to him, even
though he himself sits in Paris. There is only one problem:
How does a cat cross a river? And this is what occurred to
me: On the exchange there is a bird called Todros. This
very Todros used to be a great big speculator, a red-hot
speculator, fire and brimstone! After the crisis which
shook the world, all the big speculators (and me in the
middle) became brokers, whereupon Todros went off to
Paris and started manipulating huge deals worth millions. My luck that Todros is now back in Yehupetz! As

soon as I learned this, I took the trouble to dash to his home at once and give him a proper detailed account of how I smelled out a place in the Caucasus where oil is squirting, and since a lot of money is asked for it, it looks as if the deal is suitable only for Paris. Says Todros to me, "I have a buyer for it!" So I ask him, "Who is your buyer?" Says he, "Rothschild!" "Do you actually know Rothschild?" I ask him. "Do I know Rothschild! May you and I have half as much in our pockets as I've already earned from doing business with him!" "Please excuse me," I say, "but would it be too much trouble for you to write to Rothschild in Paris?" "Writing," says he, "is no trick at all. We may be good pals, but business is business. One has to have a specification and a plan—otherwise, nothing can be done."

To make a long story short, I went off to my partners, got the specification from them and everything that goes with it, and brought them to Todros. Well, my dearest wife, how do you like the way Menahem-Mendl conducts business with the help of God? If only the Almighty cooperates, as soon as the good news comes from Rothschild, just imagine what the rest of the big Yehupetz brokers will look like alongside of me!

In the meantime, the only trouble is that I haven't got a penny to my name. You ought to see what's going on here —we are all pinched for money. Everybody is absolutely dying for a kopeck. Any day now we are expecting terrific bankruptcies. But you are not to worry, my dearest wife, everything in its own good time. For all our trials and tribulations we shall be rewarded with plenty of joy, God willing. Just let the good news come from Paris with the grace of God, and I'll make a beeline to the shops and take care of myself and of you and of all the children, God bless them. And since I am busy and pressed for time, I must cut this short. Please God, in my next letter I'll write you everything in detail. For the time being, may the Lord grant health and success. Greet the children, God bless them, and give my kindest regards to everyone, to old and young, to big and small.

From me, your husband,
Menahem-Mendl.

J u s t   r e m e m b e r e d! As for what you ask about Dreyfus, that's a very pretty story, indeed. This is how it goes. It seems that in Paris there was a Captain Dreyfus; that is, a captain who was called Dreyfus. There was also Esterhazy who was a major. (A major is bigger than a captain, or maybe it's the other way around—a captain is bigger than a major.) Anyhow, he was a Jew—Dreyfus, I mean. And Esterhazy, the major, was not a Jew. So he went and wrote a *bordereau*. I mean, Major Esterhazy wrote the *bordereau* and saddled Dreyfus with it. So Dreyfus went and attempted to clear himself. So they tried him and condemned him to sit forever on an island in the middle of the sea, all alone by himself. Then Zola came along; he raised a rumpus and showed with proofs that he knew absolutely for sure that it wasn't Dreyfus who wrote the *bordereau*—what do you want of him?—it was all the work of that Major Esterhazy! So then they went and tried him, and they made him sit, too. But he—Zola, I mean—managed to run away. So along comes somebody else, Picquart by name (this one was a colonel) , and he also started yelling and shouting. Then appeared Mercier—that one was even a general!—and another man called Roget (another general) and many more generals, and all of them gave false witness against Dreyfus. So then the Frenchies raised a great hullabaloo demanding that he be brought back—Dreyfus, I mean. So back he came, and he was tried in a court in Rennes. Then an advocate came from Paris. They wanted to shoot him—as a matter of fact, they did shoot him in the back—but he made hash of all the generals. Nevertheless, Dreyfus was tried again; only they let him go immediately. That is, he was judged guilty and not guilty—make of that what you will! . . . Is the story about Dreyfus quite clear to you now?

As above.

22

Sheineh-Sheindl from Kasrilevka to her husband, Menahem-Mendl, in Yehupetz

To my dear, esteemed, renowned, and honored husband, the wise and learned Menahem-Mendl, may his light shine forever.

In the first place, I want to let you know that we are all, praise the Lord, perfectly well, and may we hear the same from you, please God, and never anything worse.

In the second place, I am writing to say, my dearest husband, that there is little to choose between you and a madman. All you need is to start running around the streets with a broom in your hand. Has anyone heard the like?! He's squirting oil, flying to Paris, scattering millions! He thinks he's as good as any Yehupetz millionaire—they have no money, and he hasn't a kopeck either. As Mother says, God bless her, "When it comes to giving up the ghost, there's no difference between a white goat and a black one. . . ."

Remember my words, Mendl: You'll be brought home either in chains or in a nightshirt, and it will serve you right! Maybe then you'll recall that you have a wife till a hundred and twenty years who has more sense than you. As for the gifts you intend to buy me, I thank you very kindly for them. God help Yehupetz merchants if they have customers like you and your partners, those liars who earn billions and starve for a penny, and may this not be the worst of it, which is the heartfelt wish of your really devoted wife,

Sheineh-Sheindl.

As for that story about Dreyfus which you explained to me, may I know misery in my life, if I know what you're talking about! How can a Jew become a captain, and what is that *bondero* which they keep tossing from one to another? Why did Zola have to run away, and why would they want to shoot him—and if they did shoot him, why shoot him in the back and not the front? As Mother says, God bless her, "He that knows a little is quick to repeat it. . . ."

23

Menahem-Mendl from Yehupetz to his wife,
Sheineh-Sheindl, in Kasrilevka

To my dear, wise, and modest helpmeet, Sheineh-Sheindl,
long may she live!

Firstly, I am come to inform you that I am, by the
grace of God, well and in good cheer. May the Lord,
blessed be His name, grant that we always hear from one
another none but the best, the most comforting, and the
happiest of tidings—amen.

And Secondly, I want you to know, my dearest
wife, that I wish the earth had swallowed up the Caucasus before I ever heard of it. I cannot even show my face
on the exchange any longer. What is the story? It's a very
simple story. Yesterday I come to the exchange, and I find
Todros there. He says to me, "Look here, mister, where
exactly is that Caucasus of yours?" "Caucasus," I say to
him, "is in the Caucasus. Why, what's the matter?" Says
he, "I took a look at the map to find the town where your
oil wells are supposed to be, and all I could find was moonshine." "What do you mean, moonshine?" I ask. "I mean,"
says he, "that there is no such town on the face of the earth.
Evidently the name comes from a fairy tale. How can anyone," says he, "make a proposition which was unbegotten
and unborn? And to whom! To Rothschild! Do you know,"
he says, "who Rothschild is?" "Why shouldn't I know?"
say I. "I know very well who Rothschild is, but why blame

me?" I say, "I didn't invent Caucasus. I simply told *you* what they told *me*." So I immediately dashed off to look for the Cape. I found him in the Jewish Dairy where all the Jews spend their days, and I took him to task at once: "Tell me, my dear Mr. Cape, where is our proposition actually?" "What a question!" says he. "Isn't the proposition in your hands? You have the buyer!" "No," I say, "that's not what I mean. I mean the proposition itself. Where is it tucked away—in what part of the country, how does one get to it, and what's the name of the town?" "That," says he, "I cannot tell you. Probably my partner knows." So we both go looking for his partner. But his partner says he got the proposition from Red-Nose. Red-Nose says he hasn't the slightest idea—all he knows is what Thick-Lips said. He said that Mr. Cape had a business in Caucasus, but what Caucasus, which Caucasus, he doesn't know—would that he knew less of misery!

In short, when we tried to get to the bottom of it and trace the source of the whole business, each one pointed to the other, the other to the third—and this went on until, in the end, it turned out that apparently the fault was entirely mine. This is my usual luck, for my sins, every time and in every case, I am the scapegoat!

Do you know, my dearest wife, what conclusion I have come to? If a man has no luck, he may as well be buried alive. Whatever I put my hand to always looks good and fine and beautiful at the start—luck is almost in sight; almost it is already in my pocket—and then suddenly the wheel turns, and everything goes up in smoke! Evidently it isn't in the books that I should make money on brokerage, amass a nice pile, and retire with it. It is not in the books that Menahem-Mendl should get rich like other brokers in Yehupetz. Everyone is making a lot of noise— I alone have to stand apart and watch the whole world doing business and making money, while I make no headway, as if I were an outsider. I can see millions in front of my eyes—but I cannot touch them. . . . Always I seem to be on the other side of the fence. . . . I suppose I haven't yet pushed myself out onto the right path. Nobody knows where his luck lies. . . . You have to search a long time for it, and if you search long enough, you may find it. . . . And since I am terribly depressed, I must cut this short. Please God, in my next letter I'll write you everything in detail. My kindest regards to your father and mother, and write me how you are feeling maybe, and greet the children, God bless them, and let me know what's new with you in Kasrilevka.

From me, your husband,
Menahem-Mendl.

Just remembered! It is said that "the sorrow of many is half a consolation." When you observe the troubles of other people, your heart becomes a little lighter. For example, take the man who shares my room. Once he was a contractor, he says, a rich man, the owner of houses and shops, and now he has nothing but a lawsuit with the treasury, from which he has money coming to him, and lots of it. But since at the moment he hasn't a kopeck to his name, he is staying with me. When, please God, he wins the lawsuit, he says he won't forget me. . . . And there's that other man who is staying with us here —he's even poorer than the first. He is a writer. He writes in the papers and is composing a whole book! In the meantime, until the book is finished, he is staying with us, and out of charity the landlady sometimes gives him a glass of tea. . . . And there's still another man in our lodging house—that one is a real pauper. The writer can't hold a candle to him! Who he is and what he is—I myself do not know; something of an agent, a bit of a marriage broker, maybe an actor—he sings songs and exterminates mice— a very merry fellow, even if he hasn't a shirt to his back or a slice of bread for his supper! In short, one gets to see so much misery in the world, one forgets one's own. . . . But for heaven's sake, don't forget to write how you are feeling and all about the children, God bless them, and about your father and mother, old and young, big and small.

As above.

24

Sheineh-Sheindl from Kasrilevka to her husband, Menahem-Mendl, in Yehupetz

To my dear, esteemed, renowned, and honored husband, the wise and learned Menahem-Mendl, may his light shine forever.

In the first place, I want to let you know that we are all, praise the Lord, perfectly well, and may we hear the same from you, please God, and never anything worse.

In the second place, I am writing to say, my dearest husband, didn't I tell you so, you featherbrained dolt?! You ought to kiss every word I wrote you. As Mother says, God bless her, "Kiss the whip that beats you! . . ." So now that you've parted company with the big fish, you are getting mixed up with a fine bunch of small-fry, miserable wretches, contractors, beggars, scribblers, songwriters, mice catchers—there's nobody around to laugh with me! Certainly for their sake one has to remain in a Yehupetz lodging house and throw one's last pennies to the wind!

What I do like is that you seem to have returned to your senses: You say, evidently it wasn't written in the books that you should rise in the world and become a millionaire. Have you any doubt left, Mendl? All this time I've been screaming that you should drive those idiotic ideas out of your head. May I be proof against misery and you from foolishness, as you are from earning millions! Forget about the millions, Mendl! Forget there's a man called Brodsky. Then all will be well with you. "Look below you, and not above!" Isn't that written in some book? And don't envy those fine folk in Yehupetz who are making such a noise. Let them make a noise! Let them crackle and rattle, let them crash and smash, and let them burst into little pieces, which is the heartfelt wish of your really devoted wife,

Sheineh-Sheindl.

I'd like to know one thing: Why did you, my darling Mendl, suddenly remember to ask about our Kasrilevka? And how is it that I've suddenly become so precious to you that you've started worrying about my health? It almost seems you're really beginning to miss us! . . . As Mother says, God bless her, "Let the calf run loose— when it gets hungry, it will find its way home. . . ." I am waiting for a telegram telling me you are coming home. It's time you did—it's high time, and God grant this be my last letter. . . .

Book IV

A RESPECTABLE OCCUPATION

Menahem-Mendl, Writer

I

Menahem-Mendl from Yehupetz to his wife,
Sheineh-Sheindl, in Kasrilevka

To my dear, wise, and modest helpmeet, Sheineh-Sheindl,
long may she live!

Firstly, I am come to inform you that I am, by the
grace of God, well and in good cheer. May the Lord,
blessed be His name, grant that we always hear from one
another none but the best, the most comforting, and the
happiest of tidings—amen.

And Secondly, I want you to know, my dearest
wife, that I am finished with business. It's all over and
done with—off with the exchange, off with Semedeni, off
with brokerage! It's all nothing but a barefaced swindle,
a scramble, a blight, a crying shame! I have a brand-new
profession now—I have chosen an occupation which is
much more decent, much more respectable. You can congratulate me: I have become a writer. I am writing! But
you'll probably want to know how I came to writing. Well,
it came from on high.

If you recall from my last letter, in the lodging house
where I am staying I met a writer who writes for the
newspapers and actually makes a living at it. How is that?
Well, he simply sits down at a table, writes something,
sends it off, and then it gets printed. And after it is
printed, he is paid by the line—a kopeck a line—as many
kopecks as there are lines. So I thought it over: For heav-

en's sake, am I any worse than he, goodness me? Does it take such a lot of learning? If you ask me, I have also studied in a *heder,* and as a matter of fact, my handwriting 'is much prettier than his—so why shouldn't I make a stab at it and write something for a Yiddish paper? What's there to be afraid of? No one will have my head for it! There are only two alternatives: Either they'll accept it, or else they'll reject it!

So I went and wrote a letter directly to *Gazette.* Thus and so, I wrote, telling them my whole biography. How I used to be a big shot on the exchange in Odessa and in Yehupetz, how I served all sorts of strange gods, dealt in London and in papers, and in hausses and baisses, to the tune of millions of rubles, how seven and seventy times I was on the top, and then on the very bottom—rich to-day, poor tomorrow; today a millionaire, tomorrow a pauper. In short, I spared no effort in describing everything in detail, covering maybe ten sheets of paper. I asked them to let me know whether they liked my style of writing, for I was ready to write and write and write.

And you suppose that a month and a half later I didn't receive a reply from *Gazette? Gazette* writes they rather like the way I write and proposes that I write detailed articles for them, and if my articles are well written, they will be glad to print them in their paper and pay me by the line, a kopeck a line. Do you understand? As many kopecks as there are lines. So I immediately picked up my pen to figure out how much I can manage to write. I calculated that on a long summer's day I could manage to write not less than a thousand lines. Now, doesn't that add up to a tenner a day? Ten rubles a day would therefore come to almost three hundred a month. Not a bad salary, what do you think? And in order not to waste time, I bought a bottle of ink and a ream of paper and sat down to

work. And since I am busy writing, I must cut this short.
Please God, in my next letter I'll write you everything
in detail. For the time being, may the Lord grant health
and success. Greet the children, God bless them, and give
my kindest regards to your father and mother, to old and
young, to big and small.

From me, your husband,
Menahem-Mendl.

Just remembered! If the Lord is good enough
to help me finish with my writing—that is to say, with
the title to my article (because I still haven't found a name
for it) —I'll post it off to *Gazette* at once and ask them to
send a few rubles on account in your name to Kasrilevka.
I should like, my dearest wife, that you too should have
some pleasure from my present occupation. I think it is
rather more decent than brokerage—in brokerage, your
earnings are called commission; in writing, they're called
honorarium. . . . And oh, how sweet, how easy and how
respectable, this honorarium! . . .

As above.

2

Sheineh-Sheindl from Kasrilevka to her husband, Menahem-Mendl, in Yehupetz

To my dear, esteemed, renowned, and honored husband, the wise and learned Menahem-Mendl, may his light shine forever.

In the first place, I want to let you know that we are all, praise the Lord, perfectly well, and may we hear the same from you, please God, and never anything worse.

In the second place, I am writing to ask, my dearest, beloved husband: What will be the end of you?! There is no bullet made to your size. One cannot get at you either with good or with ill. One may as well shoot at a blank wall! Mother, God bless her, should have her sayings recorded. "An invalid," she says, "will leave his sickbed; a drunkard will sober up; a dark man will change his skin; but a fool will remain a fool forever. . . ." Are you going to tell me she isn't right? Just think about everything you've managed to do since I've known you as a husband, worse luck for me! And if that weren't bad enough, you go and turn into a clown in your old age—you become an ink slinger, a scribbler, a writer! A writer writing particles. And there are actually fools who pay for them! Heaven knows what mischief you're capable of brewing with your writing, God forbid. As for me, I've already learned my bitter lesson. As Mother says, God bless her, "Don't show a whip to a beaten dog. . . ." Always he manages to think up an easy job for himself—beautiful castles in the air! Have you heard the like? He will stay in his lodging house in Yehupetz and scribble particles, while I am rotting away in Kasrilevka with his children and wasting away with fluenza! It is now three weeks since she broke into our house, that cursed fluenza, and she refuses to leave. She has had a fling at everybody, big and small. . . .

And as for your giving me alms out of your writings, I thank you in advance for it. May your fine Yehupetz friends have as much to pay for their breakfast with as what I expect you to receive as a horrorarium. I've got enough horror and misery without it. . . . And if you don't want me to part with this world in the prime of my youth and turn your children into orphans, God forbid, you must drive out of your head all those occupations which you are fashioning out of air, and all your wonderful scribbles, and come home sometime to your wife and children, to your father-in-law and your mother-in-law, and then, God willing, you'll be a welcome guest in our house. As Mother says, God bless her, "Even a one-eyed husband is a husband . . ." which is the heartfelt wish of your really devoted wife,

Sheineh-Sheindl.

Do you remember Moishe-Dovid, the *Litvak?* Quite some time ago he decided to get rid of his wife with whom he wasn't getting along, but he didn't know how. So off he went to America. So off she went after him, nabbed him at the frontier, and raised such a racket that he immediately gave in and returned to Kasrilevka with his tail between his legs. But what can you expect of a Litvak? Let all my troubles fall on his head!

3

Menahem-Mendl from Yehupetz to his wife,
Sheineh-Sheindl, in Kasrilevka

To my dear, wise, and modest helpmeet, Sheineh-Sheindl,
long may she live!

F i r s t l y, I am come to inform you that I am, by the
grace of God, well and in good cheer. May the Lord,
blessed be His name, grant that we always hear from one
another none but the best, the most comforting, and the
happiest of tidings—amen.

A n d S e c o n d l y, I want you to know, my dearest
wife, that the Lord willing, everything is going to be fine.
I have been, thank God, already printed in the paper
right along with other writers, and now I feel quite a different man. The first time I saw my name—MENAHEM-
MENDL—printed in the paper, tears actually came to my
eyes. And do you know why? Just because of all that kind-
ness! To think that there are such fine, good people in the
world! I am talking about *Gazette*. Common sense tells
me that I am probably not the only pebble on their
beach—there must be plenty of other writers besides me.
Nevertheless, they took the trouble to sit down and read
my writing, and it would seem that they've read it from
the first page to the very last, and they actually replied to
me in public—that is, in the column called "Editor's An-
swers," saying they liked my writing—only it's a bit on
the long side. That is number one. Number two is that

they tell me not to invent stories out of my head; what they want me to do is to paint (their own word) life in the city of Yehupetz and all the *types* one finds there. I suppose they want to know what's going on with us in Yehupetz—otherwise, what do they mean by "types"? . . . Isn't that tactful of *Gazette*? Well, one cannot be rude and delay one's answer till tomorrow. So I took off my coat and sat down to write to them, and today is the third day that I'm writing—I am writing and writing, and the writing doesn't seem to stop! And since I am very busy writing and pressed for time, I must cut this short. Please God, in my next letter I'll write you everything in detail. For the time being, may the Lord grant health and success. Greet the children, God bless them, and give my kindest regards to your father and mother, to old and young, to big and small.

From me, your husband,
Menahem-Mendl.

Just remembered! Please let me know whether you've received a little something from *Gazette*. Because I've asked them to send you some money on account for the time being. What does it matter—a little more, a little less? I'll square accounts with them later.

As above.

4

Sheineh-Sheindl from Kasrilevka to her husband, Menahem-Mendl, in Yehupetz

To my dear, esteemed, renowned, and honored husband, the wise and learned Menahem-Mendl, may his light shine forever.

In the first place, I want to let you know that we are all, praise the Lord, perfectly well, and may we hear the same from you, please God, and never anything worse.

In the second place, I am writing to say, my dearest husband, that your letters are again making me spit blood. Who is that beauty of yours, in whose honor you remove your coat and with whom you seem to be so lovey-dovey? Let her burn to an ash together with her money! I don't need any of her favors. As Mother says, God bless her, "Don't give me your honey, and keep the sting to yourself." But I'm sure your *Gazette* will have a long spell of illness before she sends me a kopeck. Well, *I* don't give a kopeck for all the writings you write me in your letters! But if it's in the books that my husband *must* be a writer, I cannot understand why you have to stay in Yehupetz for it? Isn't there any ink in Kasrilevka?

I'm sure there is something behind all this, some jiggery-pokery. As Mother says, God bless her, "Bite into an apple, and you are bound to find a worm. . . ." Therefore, my dearest husband, please collect all your writings and come home without any further excuses, because I can no longer bear to see the children's grief. They keep asking me, "When is Papa coming home?" And I keep putting them off from Passover to Succot, and from Succot to Passover. Especially Moishe-Hersheli, God bless him— what a clever child! Much smarter than his father, which is the heartfelt wish of your really devoted wife,

Sheineh-Sheindl.

What do you say to my Braindl?! She is divorcing her second husband already! And nobody knows why. But in private he showed me black and blue marks on his arm. He is ready, he says, to wash his hands of all her dowry and jewelry, as long as he gets rid of that scourge! As Mother says, God bless her, "An ounce of luck is better than a pound of gold. . . ." None of our family seems to have any luck with their husbands. . . .

5

Menahem-Mendl from Yehupetz to his wife, Sheineh-Sheindl, in Kasrilevka

To my dear, wise, and modest helpmeet, Sheineh-Sheindl, long may she live!

F i r s t l y, I am come to inform you that I am, by the grace of God, well and in good cheer. May the Lord, blessed be His name, grant that we always hear from one another none but the best, the most comforting, and the happiest of tidings—amen.

A n d S e c o n d l y, I want you to know, my dearest wife, that I have already used up two bottles of ink and started on the third. It's quite a job to describe a city like Yehupetz! I started with the lodging house where I'm staying and first of all tackled my landlady. You'll probably ask, why the landlady? Because there's no landlord! She has been a widow for the past thirteen years. Her husband was a soldier, and she was his second wife. She took him, she says, because of his position, in order to get permission to live in Yehupetz, and, she says, she can wish only on her worst enemies the kind of life she led with him, because she was a good twenty years younger than he. When she was young, she says, she was as pretty as a picture; all the young men, Jew and non-Jew alike, were crazy about her. . . . And now she has to sit and wait till Menahem-Mendl decides to have a plate of *borshch* occasionally or a piece of meat with horseradish. And on this she is supposed to support a son and a daughter who go to high school, lazybones both of them, who won't lift a finger to help her and who expect Mama to wait on them hand and foot—in the morning a glass of coffee in bed, and when they come home from school, nobody asks whether there is or there isn't anything to eat; lunch has to be ready on the table; otherwise they are liable to raise the roof. That's the kind of children they are. The other day her daughter got up in the morning and started screaming that there was no soap to wash with. When the dining room was full of guests, sitting around the table drinking tea, she burst in half-naked, her chest exposed, shouting at her mother in Russian, "It's absolutely disgusting!" This was too much for us, and we started to scold her: Is that what they are teaching her at school? "Bad enough," say I, "that your mother wears herself to the bone, polishing your boots while you're asleep. . . ." I was just about to give her a good lecture, when that youngster—her brother—pipes up, "What business is it of yours?! . . ." and starts giving me a piece of his mind, the impudence! This touched me so to the quick that I went and wrote a full description of the wretched widow and her precious children, and I trust that when it's printed, it will serve them better than a lesson.

The world is such a large place! There must be many such widows and many such children who go to high school and vex their poor mothers to death. . . . Now, do you understand, my dearest wife, why they pay me money for writing? And since I am very busy and pressed for time, I must cut this short. Please God, in my next letter I'll write you everything in detail. For the time being, may the Lord grant health and success. Greet the children,

God bless them, and give my kindest regards to your father and mother, to old and young, to big and small.

From me, your husband,
Menahem-Mendl.

Just remembered! From your remarks about *Gazette,* I see you don't quite understand what *Gazette* is. It is not a single person, but a number of people who got together in order to publish a newspaper. The paper is sent to all the cities and is sold for cash. But since a paper requires material, *Gazette* requests us to write, and they pay us for it. As for us, we do as they request—that is, we write, while they print. Do you understand what kind of business it is now?

As above.

6

Sheineh-Sheindl from Kasrilevka to her husband, Menahem-Mendl, in Yehupetz

To my dear, esteemed, renowned, and honored husband, the wise and learned Menahem-Mendl, may his light shine forever.

In the first place, I want to let you know that we are all, praise the Lord, perfectly well, and may we hear the same from you, please God, and never anything worse.

In the second place, I am writing to say, my dearest husband, that I've read your letter and couldn't believe my eyes. This cannot be anything but a nightmare; can't you find anything better to write about? The good Lord has blessed him with a widow who has a couple of beastly children—so his heart melts and he makes a terrible fuss over her! If I were in Yehupetz and in your shoes, I'd describe that young whippersnapper differently, and as for that wench with naked shoulders, I'd shut her up in the kitchen and make her sit on a bench and peel potatoes, instead of reading lectures to her! . . .

Well, well, my husband has become a lecturer, a preacher, and what's more, he says he gets paid for it! As Mother says, God bless her, "It takes all kinds of madmen to make a world. . . ." Seems to me that instead of peeking into other people's pots and getting mixed up with their children, you would do better to worry your head

over your own. Are you a father to your children, or aren't
you? You ought to hear Moishe-Hersheli recite the al-
phabet—your Yehupetz widow and your *Gazette* could
both answer for his sins. If I were in better spirits, I'd
have his picture taken with the other children and send
it to you so as to show you whom you've swapped for widows, *Gazettes,* and other kind of plagues and tribulations,
which is the heartfelt wish of your really devoted wife,

Sheineh-Sheindl.

7

Menahem-Mendl from Yehupetz to his wife,
Sheineh-Sheindl, in Kasrilevka

To my dear, wise, and modest helpmeet, Sheineh-Sheindl,
long may she live!

F i r s t l y, I am come to inform you that I am, by the
grace of God, well and in good cheer. May the Lord,
blessed be His name, grant that we always hear from one
another none but the best, the most comforting, and the
happiest of tidings—amen.

A n d S e c o n d l y, I want you to know, my dearest
wife, that I have already finished with the landlady and
started on the guests in the lodging house. That is to say,
I am describing all the luckless wretches who live under
the same roof with me. I don't mind boasting that I've
been most successful, knock on wood. There is no shortage
of wretches here—each one is more miserable than the
next. But the worst wretch of all is the one we call Lucky.
There is so much to write about him, there isn't enough
paper and ink. This young fellow comes from the town of
Shvanetz. He made his first marriage in the town of Ladi-
zhin, the second in Soroki. He settled in Yekaterinoslav,
and there he launched his first business: He started dealing in gold. That is to say, a group of rascals sold him several bags of gold dust and took from him every penny he
possessed. After they made off, he discovered that the bags
were filled with dust—only it wasn't gold dust.

He felt so bad about this that he was ready to throw himself alive into the Dnieper River. But what did he do instead? He took his cane and went on the stock exchange. There he joined one mountain to another, as the saying goes; he made a few shekels and put an advertisement in the newspapers saying that he was looking for a business with a partner. It didn't take long before he unearthed a partner with an iron business—that is, together they bought a piece of land near Krivoy Rog, rich in iron ore. They had an offer of several thousands in goodwill money for it, but he said, "Half a million, or nothing!" So he got nothing. Then he switched over to coal mining. He got hold of a German engineer (that is, a Jew who spoke German), and they rented a mine—at a fair price, too. But when they started digging for coal, an underground spring of water burst open. Nobody knew where it came from, but it turned into a deluge. So they put two people to pump the water out. The more they pumped, the more water came up—the story had no end. So he washed his hands of the German and got together with a man who buys up stale cracked eggs and makes something out of the yolks—I forget what it's called. Well, it was his good luck—the machine burst. The man took to his heels and left him all alone with the stale eggs. The eggs started to smell so high that the police came and threatened to arrest him. So in the middle of the night he had to jump out of a window to make his getaway, and he let the city of Yekaterinoslav worry about the eggs.

He had a little money, so he went to Kremenchug and together with a partner opened a factory for making cigarette wrappers. Well, he had to pick out a partner who was crazy about chess, and since he is also crazy about chess (he says he can play chess day and night, without eating, sleeping, or drinking), the two of them did nothing but play chess until they found they had nothing but empty boxes left. What happened to the wrappers, nobody knows.

In the meantime, he heard that some pharmacist in a small town nearby was selling his shop and everything he owned at half price—a real, honest-to-goodness bargain. So off he went and bought it lock, stock, and barrel at half price and started packing it up. He could have made a fortune on it. But as luck would have it, among the various wares there was also a box of gunpowder. And when the entire stock was in the railway wagon, the gunpowder started shooting. It shot all through the wagon and shot a foot off the conductor. He himself just managed to get away with his life.

Well, what do you say to Lucky? He himself says that when he looks into a river, every fish gives up its ghost. As you see, he is full of such quips, as if he didn't have his share of misfortune. To look at him—he is nothing much: He is small, lively, and has little burning eyes. His cap is always at the back of his head, his hands are always in his pockets, and his brain is constantly humming with plots and plans and combinations without end!

He says he absolutely has to become a millionaire— otherwise, he'll up and go to America. There, he says, he won't have a thing to worry about. He is trying to talk me into going to America with him. He says people like us can't get lost anywhere. But I'd have to be crazy to give up such a respectable business as writing in order to look for luck on the other side of the ocean! And since I am very busy and pressed for time, I must cut this short. Please God, in my next letter, I'll write you everything in detail. For the time being, may the Lord grant health and success. Greet the children, God bless them, and give my kindest regards to your father and mother, to old and young, to big and small.

From me, your husband,
Menahem-Mendl.

J u s t   r e m e m b e r e d! I cannot understand why I haven't received any reply from *Gazette* about the first piece of work I sent them. No reply and no money. I have already written them three letters. I figure, if not today, then tomorrow, please God, I ought to have an answer from them.

As above.

8

Sheineh-Sheindl from Kasrilevka to her husband, Menahem-Mendl, in Yehupetz

To my dear, esteemed, renowned, and honored husband, the wise and learned Menahem-Mendl, may his light shine forever.

In the first place, I want to let you know that we are all, praise the Lord, perfectly well, and may we hear the same from you, please God, and never anything worse.

In the second place, I am writing to say, my dearest husband, that the moment you receive this letter you must, in the name of God, return home at once because my poor father is mortally ill. The doctors have already made a council, and they found—woe to all of us!—that he has water in his belly. It is heartrending to watch his suffering. And as you can imagine, it's hard to recognize Mother, God bless her! Everyone can see she is absolutely sacrificing herself for him. She says, "You can get used even to an old pot if you spend thirty years under the same roof with it. . . ." And there you are, sitting pretty in your wonderful Yehupetz, writing about all kinds of wretches, may they be the scapegoats for my father's smallest finger, which is the heartfelt wish of your really devoted wife,

Sheineh-Sheindl.

Don't forget! In God's name, leave Yehupetz at once, and dash off a telegram to me!

9

Menahem-Mendl from Yehupetz to his wife,
Sheineh-Sheindl, in Kasrilevka

To my dear, wise, and modest helpmeet, Sheineh-Sheindl,
long may she live!

F i r s t l y, I am come to inform you that I am, by the
grace of God, well and in good cheer. May the Lord,
blessed be His name, grant that we always hear from one
another none but the best, the most comforting, and the
happiest of tidings—amen.

A n d S e c o n d l y, I want you to know, my dearest
wife, that your letter was like a bullet straight into my
heart. If I had wings, I'd fly to Kasrilevka like an eagle.
But I cannot stir because I haven't got the wherewithal. I
owe so much money to my landlady that I don't own
the hair on my head. Not only have I eaten her out of
house and home, but I borrowed from her to pay for paper and ink. I kept constantly thinking: a little while
longer. . . . So much paper and ink were used up, so
many beautiful stories invented—all my fingers worn to
the bone, and *Gazette* doesn't reply! They put a padlock
on their lips; that isn't nice of them at all! They ought to
make up their minds: You don't like my writings? So why
not write and tell me to stop writing? Why make a man
sweat for nothing? Anyone else in my place would give
them a good dressing down. Or if I had money, I'd send
them a telegram: "DO OR DIE." I'm simply in no condition

to describe my vexation, my misery and depression. I cannot even lift my pen to write about it. Just imagine, I asked them at least to send me their paper free of charge —and there's no reply to that either. Had I spent all this time chopping wood, I'm sure I would have earned more. I don't know how it is with other writers, but I know they treated me like dirt. "I will lift up mine eyes unto the hills, from whence cometh my help. . . ." Perhaps the Almighty will help me, because "I am come into deep waters where the floods overflow me . . ." and nothing can be worse than that. . . . And since I am terribly depressed, I must cut this short. Please God, in my next letter I'll write you everything in detail. For the time being, may the Lord grant health, success, and speedy recovery to your father. May we see everyone well and strong, God willing, including the children, whom I miss terribly —I am absolutely sick with longing for them!

From me, your husband,
Menahem-Mendl.

Just remembered! This letter has been lying around for two days because I haven't any money for postage. I keep thinking over and over again: Where to turn, what to do, where to begin? Seems to me there isn't any business left I haven't tried my hand at. There is only one thing I have passed over, so far: matchmaking. There is a marriage broker staying in my rooming house, and to judge from the stories he tells, he is making a fortune. This business may not be as respectable as writing, but it is certainly more decent than brokerage. The main thing is—if only the Almighty were to send a bit of luck my way!

As above.

10

To my dear, esteemed, renowned, and honored husband, the wise and learned Menahem-Mendl, may his light shine forever.

In the first place, I want to let you know that we are all, praise the Lord, perfectly well, and may we hear the same from you, please God, and never anything worse.

In the second place, I am writing to say that I have nothing to say to you. I showed your letter to Mother, and she says it's all my fault. "As you make your bed, so must you lie in it," she says. . . . "Had you allowed me to write to that treasure of yours," she says, "I would have had him here long ago. I would have taken the trouble," she says, "to go after him. It's lucky for you," says she, "that Father is on his deathbed, and neither of us can stand on our feet. . . ."

The money I'm sending you with this letter is my mother's. Never forget the goodness of her heart! And I beg the good Lord to keep me from receiving any more of your sweet letters, and as soon as you leave Yehupetz, may the earth open and swallow that city, like Sodom and Gomorrah, together with all its golden business deals, its fortunes, its brokers, its matchmakers, lodging houses, landladies and *Gazettes,* which is the heartfelt wish of your really devoted wife,

Sheineh-Sheindl.

Book V

NO LUCK!

Menahem-Mendl, Marriage Broker

Menahem-Mendl from the road to his wife,
Sheineh-Sheindl, in Kasrilevka

To my dear, wise, and modest helpmeet, Sheineh-Sheindl, long may she live!

Firstly, I am come to inform you that I am, by the grace of God, well and in good cheer. May the Lord, blessed be His name, grant that we always hear from one another none but the best, the most comforting, and the happiest of tidings—amen.

And Secondly, I want you to know, my dearest wife, that I have no luck. Luck simply turns its back on me, even if I tear myself into shreds. As soon as I received the few rubles you sent me, the first thing I did was to pay my debt to my landlady, and then I started getting ready for the journey. What's more, I was even sitting in the train already! I bought a ticket to Fastov, figuring to go from Fastov straight home to Kasrilevka. But we have a very great and powerful God in heaven—wait and hear what He did to me!

You may recall my writing you that one of the guests in my lodging house was a marriage broker. Leib Lebelski is his name, and he used to boast that in his breast pocket you could find all the people in the world who want to get married and that he was making a fortune. It so happened that he had to go away for a couple of days in order to arrange an important match. He said he received an urgent telegram to drop everything and to leave. So he gave a big parcel of documents to the landlady, asking her to keep it until his return, when he would square accounts with her. Maybe *you've* seen him since? *We* certainly haven't. Before I left, my landlady says to me, "You're going on the same railway line—take the marriage broker's parcel along with you; maybe you'll run into that wretch somewhere along the route; then you can return it to him." Say I, "Why give me another man's property?" Says she, "Don't be afraid—this isn't money—it's just a lot of scrap paper." And that was that.

When I was sitting in the train, I opened the parcel just out of curiosity. I took a look inside and found a whole treasure trove: letters from marriage brokers, lists of marriageable parties, and . . . just papers. Among the documents, there was a long alphabetical list of eligible men and women, written in the holy tongue. I pass it on to you, word for word:

AVRUTCH. Eva, daughter of Master Reb Levi Thinleg. . . . Terribly noble lineage. . . . Mother: Miriam-Gitl, also with a pedigree. . . . Tall as a cedar of Lebanon. . . . Comely as the rose of Sharon. . . . Four thousand . . . Wants a diploma. . . .

BALTA. Faitl, son of Master Yosif Hatmaker. . . . Enlightened youth. . . . Lover of Zion. . . . Mastered the art of bookkeeping. . . . Exempt from military service. . . . Says his prayers daily. . . . Seeks fleshpots of Egypt. . . .

DUBNO. Lea, daughter of Master Reb Meir Dumpling. . . . Good family. . . . Short in the leg. . . . Red tresses. . . . Lisps in French. . . . Comes with money. . . .

GLUCHOW. Yephim Bolosni. . . . Clean-shaven druggist, not a hair on his chin. . . . However, likes Hebrews. . . . Usurer. . . . Insists on brunette. . . .

HEISSIN. Lippe Brooch. . . . Itzi Gosling's brother-in-law. . . . Big shot in Reb Zalman's sugar refinery in Radomysl. . . . An only heir. . . . The boy is as beautiful as a doll. . . . Twinkle in his eye. . . . Wants a bucket of gold. . . .

KASRILEVKA. Reb Nathan Korah. . . . As rich as Korah. . . . A real swine. . . . Son: Yosif Itzhok. . . . Enlightened . . . Bookworm. . . . Torgenev and Darven. . . . Still waters. . . . Wants a poor orphan. . . . Peerless beauty. . . . Won't faint if forced to pay expenses. . . . "If you like to dance, you have to pay the fiddler. . . ."

KHMELNIK. Madame Basia Battleax. . . . Money-lending widow. . . . Terrific brain. . . . Wants a learned Jew. . . . Doesn't insist on shekels. . . .

KREMENCHUG. Terribly enlightened and Zionistic. . . . Hundreds of commissions. . . . Smart as a whistle. . . . Good in chess. . . . The Talmud by heart. . . . Knows a lot and has gift of gab. . . . Capital storyteller. . . . Wonderful handwriting. . . . Rumored to be married. . . .

LIPOVETS. Son of Master Leibush Gaberdine. . . . Fervent Hassid. . . . Trying to pass examination in eight classes. . . . Resides in Odessa. . . . Plays fiddle and knows holy tongue. . . . A beauty. . . .

MEDZHIBOZH. Reb Shimshon Shepsil Shimelish. . . . Widower. . . . Has duo virgins and trio thousands. . . . But must first get married himself. . . . Also demands virgin. . . .

NEMIROV. Smichik. . . . Bernard Moyseyevich. . . .

Offspring of the famous Smichiks. . . . Divorced and independent. . . . Expert gambler. . . . Strong with government officials. . . . Very fair: wants either virgin with five thousand or divorcée with ten. . . .

PRILUKI. Student Weekday. . . . Son of Master Michel Weekday. . . . Keeps head covered when indoors. . . . Doesn't write on Sabbath. . . . Wants two score thousands, not a groat less. . . . Himself willing to give half. . . .

RADOMYSL. Grandson of Reb Naftali of Radomysl. . . . Belongs to rabbinical town. . . . Sugar refinery. . . . Man of birth and worth. . . . Half Hassid, half German gentleman. . . . Short earlocks, knee-length coat. . . . Knows tongues and competent in Law. . . . Has important uncle with millions. . . . Demands beauty pedigree two hundred thousand fortepiano modesty French wig dancing Sabbath candles—a mademoiselle without cavaliers. . . .

SHPOLA. Famous capitalist, Eliahu from Chernobyl. . . . Resides in Yehupetz. . . . Big sugar and real estate broker. . . . In partnership with famous capitalist Babushka . . . One daughter. . . . Demands the moon. . . . Somebody even more learned than a doctor. . . . Exempt from military service. . . . Beautiful as Joseph the Righteous. . . . And smart as King Solomon. . . . Singing and playing on all instruments. . . . Family tree without a blemish. . . . A heap of lucre. . . . All the virtues. . . . Almost a Rothschild. . . . Dashed off telegram to Radomysl.

SMELA. Madame Pearl. Divorcée with ten thousand. . . . Has to have a learned commissionaire. . . .

TALNI. Rabbi Reb Avremeleh Finely. . . . Widower. . . . Pious and learned. . . . Looking for widow with business. . . .

TOMASHPOL. Five virgins. . . . Three beauties, two scarecrows. . . . But give each and all either doctor with office and furniture or lawyer with practice in Yehupetz. . . . Wrote several letters. . . .

TSARITSYN. Specification of rich widower Fishmonger. . . . Resides in Astrakhan. . . . Promises two government loan tickets (first issue) besides matchmakers' commissions. . . . Must write him another (1) letter. . . .

VINNITSA. Haim Herring. . . . Plays on stock market. . . . Rides in carriage. . . . Big moneymaker. . . . Worth a price above rubies. . . .

YAMPOL. Moishe-Nissl Kimbak. . . . Brand-new rich man—Wife: Madame Beile-Lea. . . . Dying to marry off. . . . Undertakes to double other party's stake. . . . Will pay marriage broker's fees immediately dishes are broken. . . . Extra gifts to brokers from Madame. . . .

YANATOVKA. Reb Mendeleh Shovel, landlord. . . . Graybeard over seventy. . . . But pretty firm in the flesh. . . . Buried trio wives. . . . Wants virgin. . . .

ZHITOMIR. The Very Honorable Shlomo-Zalman Wheelbarrow. . . . Duo virgins. . . . Both ultra beauties. . . . The younger slightly pockmarked. . . . Piano German French. . . . Demands learning. . . . Diploma not essential. . . .

So here I am, sitting in the train with the marriage broker's parcel. Over and over again I read this list of would-be brides and would-be bridegrooms, and I think to myself: Creator of all things, how many various occupations hast thou created for thy children of Israel! Take matchmaking, for example. What can possibly be more decent, more respectable, easier, and cleaner than this profession? What's there to do? All you need is a screw in your head to enable you cleverly to figure out who would suit whom. For instance, here you have AVRUTCH with a beautiful girl with four thousand rubles who wants a diploma. On the other hand, there is BALTA with an educated Zionist who finished bookkeeping and wants money. Isn't this a perfect match? Or let us take TALNI. In this town there lives a widower who is looking for a widow with a business. So why shouldn't he take the trouble to go to KHMELNIK and take the widow Basia Battleax who wants a widower without money, as long as he is a scholar? . . .

Listen, my dearest wife, all you have to know is how to arrange combinations. Had I been born a matchmaker, I'd have put the entire trade on a different footing. I'd get in touch with all the marriage brokers in the world; I'd collect all their lists, and then I'd sit over them and start matching up (first on paper, to be sure) *this* prospective bride with *that* prospective groom and *that* prospective bride with *this* prospective groom. And in every town I would have a partner—as many partners as there are towns. At all events, whatever the fee, we would share it equally: half for me, half for him. It might even be worthwhile to open an office in Yehupetz or in Odessa and hire people to spend all their time writing letters and dashing off telegrams—whereas I, myself, would do nothing but sit, match up couples, and make combinations!

Such were the thoughts, fancies, and combinations which flitted through my head, when some wild wind blew a character into my compartment. He was completely overgrown with hair; he was dragging a sack and puffing like a goose, when he turned to me very politely, speaking in an extraordinary style: "Young man," he says. "Permit me to address you. It stands to reason that you might be good enough to take the trouble," says he, "to move your limbs somewhat to the side," says he, "so that such a man as myself, for example, might have the honor to sit beside you for a few minutes in comfort." "Why not? The honor is all mine!" say I to him, making room for him. And then, just to be polite, I ask, "Where does a Jew come from?" "In other words, you want to know wherefrom I hail? From Korets," he replies. "My name is Osher, and I am known to everyone as Reb Osher the Matchmaker. Take a good look at me," he says. "By the grace of God, I have plied the trade of matchmaking for close to forty years, in my quiet way." "Is that so!" say I. "That is to say, you are also a matchmaker?" "In other words," says he, "we are given to understand that you probably are a matchmaker for certain. To wit, we are brethren-in-arms—so according to the Law, you are entitled to a how-do-you-do!" Thus the matchmaker, thrusting a huge, soft, hairy hand at me. Then he asks (also out of politeness, I suppose), "What may your honorable name be?" Say I, "Menahem-Mendl. . . ." "The name sounds familiar," he says to me. "I've heard it somewhere but can't recall where. Well, Reb Menahem-Mendl, listen carefully to what I have to say to you," says he. "Since the Almighty in His infinite wisdom and goodness has guided our steps and arranged that we two matchmakers," says he, "should find ourselves in the same boat," says he, "perhaps it would stand to reason if, right here, on the move though we are—indeed on this very spot—we were to come to some proper arrangement." "For example," say I, "what kind of proper arrangement have you in mind? . . ." "Perhaps," says he, "you know of any lover of good wine in a cracked bottle?" "For example," say I, "what do you call good wine in a cracked bottle?" "Bear with me," says he, "and I shall immediately explain everything to you clearly and translate it for you, word by word. However, you must grant me your complete attention—I need your brains. I have," says he, "a piece of first-class merchandise in Yarmelinetz—really something special. Reb Itzikl Tashratz is his name. As far as his ancestry is concerned—we can just take it for granted. Let's put it this way: He is simply bathed in blue blood. And if it isn't enough for you that *he* comes from a good family, you may as well know that *she* comes from a still better one —his wife, I mean. The only fly in the ointment is," says he, "that he demands a lot of hard cash for his family tree. Whatever he offers, he wants the other party to double the stake. . . ." "Just one moment!" say I, "I believe I have exactly the article you require." I take my bag, find my matchmaker's notebook, look up YAMPOL and show it to him. "Here it is—just the thing you're looking for," I say. "Read it for yourself: *Moishe-Nissl Kimbak.* . . . *Brand-new rich man.* That is to say, he got rich overnight. . . . *Dying to marry off*—that is, simply bursting to get it over with. . . . *Undertakes to double other party's stake* —in other words, he's willing to give a dowry twice as big as the other party's. It is absolutely exactly what you require!"

When he heard this—and especially when he noted that Moishe-Nissl Kimbak promises to pay the brokers immediately after the dishes are broken (that is to say, right after the betrothal contract is signed), to say nothing of the extra gift his wife would give—my Reb Osher jumped from his seat, took my hand and said, "Congratulations, Reb Menahem-Mendl, our deal is closed! I have noticed," says he, "if my eyes do not deceive me, that in your basket there are egg rolls, tea, sugar, and other treasures. . . . I think it wouldn't hurt," says he, "if, for the time being, we were to say grace and when we reach Fastov safe and sound, God willing, you'll be good enough to run to the station buffet for some hot water, because," says he, "I have also noticed that you have a kettle with you, and it therefore follows that we'll be able to warm our gullets. And it may come to pass," says he, "that we might also find some spirits in the station—I fancy fifty-seven degrees in alcohol—and, incidentally, that would give us a chance to drink a toast to my Yarmelinetz nobility and your Yampol brand-new rich man who is dying to get the match over with. . . . And may it all come to pass in a happy, lucky hour!" "Amen," say I. "From your mouth into the Almighty's ear. Nevertheless," say I, "things are quicker said than done. . . ." Here the matchmaker cut me short. "Bear with me, Reb Menahem-Mendl," says he, "you don't seem to realize whom you're dealing with. You see before you neither a milksop nor a fledgling. You are talking to," says he, "a world-famous marriage broker called Reb Osher who has less hair on his head than matches which he managed to arrange by the grace of God, blessed be His name. May we both," says he, "have as many shekels in our pockets as couples whom I've married off and who have already managed to get divorced, remarried, and divorced again. . . . For me," says he, "it is sufficient to take one look at a list. The very first glance tells me whether it'll go off or not. It seems to me, your Moishe-Nissl," says he, "has a peculiar smell about him; otherwise—and let us be frank about it —why should he be so anxious about the match, and why should his wife be in such a fever to give extra gifts to the matchmakers? The inference is," says he, "that something is wrong somewhere. In other words, the apple is a wormy one. . . ." "So what would you suggest?" I ask. "I would suggest," says he, "a very simple thing: We must immediately part our ways," says he, "and each must go in a different direction. I," says he, "will go straight to Yarmelinetz to my noble Reb Itzikl Tashratz, and you to Yampol, to your Moishe-Nissl Kimbak. But take note! It must be clearly understood that each of us is to set his shoulder to

the wheel. You, on your part, must move heaven and earth
to persuade your wormy apple to give as much as possible,
whereas I, on my part," says he, "must keep a sharp look-
out that my Tashratz actually does give the entire half as
he assured me he would, because a man who trades in family trees is open to suspicion."

As you see, my dearest wife, although this started as a
joke, it seemed to turn out dead earnest. Because before
we knew it, we were in Fastov. And once in Fastov, the
first thing we did was to have some tea and an excellent
snack, and then we started discussing the deal in all seri-
ousness. I must say that at first the whole affair went against
my grain. What kind of marriage broker was I, after all?
And did I have a birthright to another man's list? Because
if you look at it one way, you might simply call it stealing!
It is as if somebody lost a wallet of money, and I picked it
up. But if you look at it another way, what's all the fuss
about? Just consider: If it comes off, we'll split the matchmakers' fees—half to me and half to Leib Lebelski. After
all, I am not a highway robber to deprive another man of
his property. In short, I thought the matter over carefully
and found that whichever way I looked at it, it was all right.

It was then decided that each of us would go his way—
he to Yarmelinetz, and I to Yampol. Our final arrangement was this: As soon as I get to Yampol, I must first try
and find out the reason why Moishe-Nissl Kimbak is so
terribly anxious for a match; then, after I've had a good
look at his home and if I am satisfied with it, I will dash off
a telegram to Reb Osher in Yarmelinetz, saying Thus and
So, and then he will dash a telegram off to me, saying So and
Thus. Afterward, we will probably all meet halfway in the
town of Zhmerinka, in order to have the parties take a
look at each other. And if they turn out to be a suitable
pair, it means it's a match!

"The important thing for you to remember," says he, "is not to economize on expenses, Reb Menahem-Mendl, and to dash off telegrams. For in matchmaking, the main thing is telegrams. . . . The moment a family sees a telegram," says he, "they get the shakes. . . ."

When it came down to business—that is, to buying railway tickets—it transpired that my world-famous marriage broker, Reb Osher, did not have a kopeck for expenses. He told me he spent his last penny on night letters and telegrams. He said, "May you earn in one month what I spend on telegrams in one week!" You see? That's the kind of business matchmaking is! To make a long story short—for in the meantime, the train does not wait—I had to lay out a few shekels for my partner, because no good business should be wrecked over expense money. We exchanged addresses, took very cordial leave of each other, and each went his way—he to Yarmelinetz, and I to Yampol.

When I came to Yampol, the first thing I did was to start prying and asking questions: Who is this man, Moishe-Nissl Kimbak? I was told, "May the likes of him be fruitful and multiply. . . ." Has he got a lot of children? I was told, "It's the poor who have a lot of children. A rich man doesn't need more than one." What kind of child has he got? I was told, "A daughter." Is she a pretty daughter? I was told, "There's enough of her for two." Is he giving a good dowry with her? I was told, "Even if he gave double, it wouldn't be enough. . . ." So I started to dig deeper: What did they mean by that? . . . I dig here, I dig there —but I can't dig anything up. So I put on my best coat and go straight to Moishe-Nissl's home.

Well, if I tried to describe his home, I couldn't manage it. It was the home of a wealthy man, crammed with all sorts of good things. And as for the people, they were jewels! When I told them who I was and why I came, they received me as if I were a prince, treated me to a glass of sweet tea, sugar biscuits, and a fragrant citron preserve, and they even put a bottle of excellent cherry brandy on the table. The father—Moishe-Nissl, I mean—won my heart immediately: a pleasant, cheerful man—one might say, a man with no gall in him. His wife—Beile-Lea, I mean—I liked her, too, from the very first glance. A handsome woman with a double chin, quiet and modest. Both of them started to pump me about the other party: Was their son a decent young man, and what were his accomplishments? What could I tell them, when I didn't have the slightest idea! But a learned Jew can always find a way out. So I turned to them and said, "Let's first finish with one party—then we'll start on the other. First of all," I said, "I want to know exactly how much you are ready to give. And second, I should like to take a look at the article in question." When he heard this—Moishe-Nissl, I mean —he turned to his wife, Beile-Lea: "Where can Sonichka be? Tell her to come here!" "Sonichka is still dressing," she said—Beile-Lea, I mean. She rose, went into the other room, and I was left alone with Moishe-Nissl.

We each took a drop of cherry brandy, tasted the citron preserve, and started chatting. What does one chat about? All sorts of things and nothing in particular. "How long have you been engaged in matchmaking?" he asks, pouring me another tot of cherry brandy. "From the day I got married," I tell him. "My father-in-law is a matchmaker; my father was a matchmaker, too, and all my brothers are matchmakers. In fact, almost all my family," I say, "is made up of matchmakers. . . ." I shoot one lie after another, without even wincing, but I feel that my face is burning. I myself don't know how all those lies got into me!

But did I have any alternative? As your mother says, "If you step into a bog, you keep sinking like a hog. . . ." But as I've already told you, I vowed to myself that should the Almighty show favor to me and I pull this deal through, I shall, God willing, divide the fee into two parts: one half for me, and the other half for the other matchmaker—Leib Lebelski, I mean—the one who left the parcel of papers in my lodging house. After all, what have I got against him? Maybe, according to law, it can be claimed that the fee belongs entirely to him. In that event, what I ask is: Where am I? After all, isn't it me who is pushing the deal through? Isn't my work worth anything? Nor, it seems to me, is it my duty to shoot off lies on behalf of someone else. And— who knows?—perhaps it was God's intention that he should lose what I would find, and in that way, thanks to me, three Jews would be able to make some money!

While I was deep in these thoughts, the door opens and in comes the mother—Beile-Lea, I mean—and right on her heels, Sonichka—I mean, the bride. Nice, big, and healthy—quite a personality, like her mother. "Well, well! what a height to her!" I think to myself. "And what a breadth to her, knock on wood! So this is Sonichka—why it's a whole ton-ichka! . . ." She, the bride, is dressed in a very outlandish way. She is wearing a funny kind of long dressing gown or wrapper, and she looks rather matronly —not because of her age, God forbid, but because of her fearful breadth. . . . Well, one must have a chat with her and find out what kind of creature she is; only he doesn't give me a chance—Moishe-Nissl, I mean. He never stops talking; he absolutely drowns me in a torrent of words. And what do you suppose he is talking about? About Yampol. He tells me what kind of town it is: a town full of hostile, envious people, gossips, snakes in the grass, every man of them ready to drown his neighbor in a teacup. . . .

And other idle words to that effect. Bless his wife—Beile-
Lea, I mean—because she interrupts him and says to her
husband, "Moishe-Nissl, maybe you've chattered enough?
Better let Sonichka play a little bit on the fortepiano."
"Have it your way," Moishe-Nissl replies and gives a nod
to his daughter. The daughter marches up to the piano, sits
down, opens a large music book, and starts pounding away
with all her might. The mother calls out to her, "Sonichka,
leave the études alone. Better play 'The Cossack Rode
Along the Dunai,' or 'Hot Buns,' or maybe even some Jewish tune. . . ." "Be good enough not to interrupt me!"
Sonichka replies in Russian and runs her fingers across the
keys so quickly that the eye cannot follow them, while
her mother's glance is riveted to her, as one might say, "Do
you see those fingers?! . . ."

And while she plays, the father and the mother slip out
of the room, and I am left alone, eye to eye with the bride
—Sonichka, I mean. "Now is the time," I think to myself,
"to have a chat with her. Let's hear whether at least she
knows how to talk." But how to begin? . . . I haven't the
remotest idea. I leave my seat, take a position behind her
broad shoulders, and say, "Excuse me if I am interrupting
your playing, Sonichka, but I want to ask you something.
. . ." She swings around on her piano stool, looks crossly
at me, and says in Russian, "For example?" "For example,"
I reply, "I should like to know what your tastes are like.
That is, what kind of husband would you prefer to have?"
"You see," she says a little more cordially, dropping her
eyes, "*actually*, I should like to have a *graduate*, but as I
know this is a *vain* hope, I should *at the very least* like him
to be *decently educated*, because even though our town
may be considered *fanatical*, nevertheless, we have all received a Russian *upbringing*, and even though we do not
attend any *educational institution*, nevertheless, you will

not find a single *mademoiselle* who is not *acquainted* with
Émile Zola, Alexander Pushkin, or even *Maxim Gorky.*
. . .*" That's what the beauty says to me—Sonichka, I
mean. She has a peculiar style of talking—half Yiddish,
half Russian—that is to say, a lot of Russian and a little
Yiddish. At this moment in comes the mother—Beile-Lea,
I mean—and calls the bride away, as if to say, "Everything
must have its limit . . ." and then the father returns—
Moishe-Nissl, I mean—and the two of us again sit down
to discuss the match: how big a dowry he is giving, where
to meet the bridegroom and his family for a onceover,
when to set the wedding date, and other details relative to
the matter in hand.

I try to get up because I want to go to the post office to
dash off a telegram, but he grabs my hand and says, "You're
not going, Reb Menahem-Mendl! you must first have supper with us—surely you must be hungry!" So we go to wash
up, and then we sit down at the table to eat and we have
cherry brandy, and throughout the entire meal, he does
not shut his mouth—Moishe-Nissl, I mean: Yampol,
Yampol, and again Yampol. . . . "You have no idea," he
says, "what a town this is! It's a town of idlers and gossips.
If you listen to me," he says, "you'll keep away from them.
Don't exchange a single word with anybody. You must not,"
he says, "tell them a thing—who you are or where you
come from or what you're doing here. And as for my name,
you must not let it pass your lips—pretend you don't even
know me. You understand, Reb Menahem-Mendl? *You
don't know me at all!*" This he repeats maybe ten times,
and then I hurry away to dash off a telegram to my partner
in Yarmelinetz, as we have agreed. I write him very
clearly, as follows: "MERCHANDISE EXAMINED. FIRST-CLASS.
SIX THOUSAND. PLEASE TELEGRAM STAKE OPPOSITE. WHERE
MEETING."

The following day I receive a very strange reply from my partner. It is apparently written in code: "PUTS FOOT DOWN ON TEN. OPPOSITE HALF SIX. ATTEMPT HITCHING UP. AGREE-ABLE ZHMERINKA. QUALITY MERCHANDISE. PLEASE TELE-GRAM."

So I run off to the father—Moishe-Nissl, I mean—show him the telegram and beg him to decode it for me because I cannot make head or tail of it. He reads it through and says, "Why, you peculiar man, what don't you understand? It's as clear as crystal. You see, he wants me to give ten, in which case the opposite side will give me half of six—in other words, three thousand. . . . Well, you can write him," he says, "that he's too clever by far. I'm going to save my breath: Whatever he gives, I'll stake twice as much. And please write him not to waste time—in those very words. Otherwise, another customer can turn up," he says.

So I follow his advice and dash off the following tele-gram to my partner: "SAVING BREATH. WHATEVER GIVES STAKING TWICE AMOUNT. DON'T WASTE TIME. ANOTHER CAN TURN UP."

Then I get another mysterious telegram from my Reb Osher: "AGREE TWICE MORE LESS ONE THOUSAND BACK. MERCHANDISE A BARGAIN."

So again I run to Moishe-Nissl with the telegram, and again he says, "It's as clear as crystal. Your partner says they are ready to stake exactly half—on one condition: They want one thousand back. To put it another way—if, for instance, I should give ten, he would be expected to give five. But as he wants a thousand back, it means that whereas I'll be giving the whole of ten, he doesn't want to give more than four. . . . Oh, what a smart man he is, your bridegroom's father!" says he. "He's trying to swindle me from top to bottom. However," he says, "I am a merchant, and I know something about business. I'd much rather give him twice as much," says he, "and throw in an extra thousand than accept from him half as much, minus a thousand less. So the calculation will go like this," he says. "If he gives three, I'll give seven; if he gives four, I'll put down nine; if he gives five, I'll lay down eleven. Have you digested this?" says he. "So go along at once," he says, "and send him an urgent telegram, telling him not to cool his heels and ask him to answer you immediately about arranging a meeting. And let's finish this business once and for all!"

I run off and dash off the following urgent telegram to my Reb Osher: "GIVES THREE LAYS SEVEN. GIVES FOUR LAYS NINE. GIVES FIVE LAYS ELEVEN. DON'T COOL HEELS. TELEGRAM URGENTLY YOU COMING."

And I receive an urgent reply, containing only two words: "COMING. COME."

And when do important telegrams arrive? In the middle of the night, naturally! No doubt you can imagine, my dearest wife, that I was unable to close an eye throughout that night. I started calculating what my share would be if, for example, I were successfully to carry through, with God's help, all the matches in the list which Leib Lebelski had lost. Is there anything too difficult for the Almighty? At any event, I firmly decided that once I see this deal through, God willing, I'll enter into a permanent partnership with Reb Osher. Because he strikes me as a very decent man— and, what's more, a successful one. And make no mistake: Leib Lebelski will not be cheated of his due, either. Have I anything against him? That wretch is also a poor man, burdened with children. . . .

I don't know how I managed to survive till daybreak. I hurried through the morning prayers and went to my bride's house to show them the telegram. They immedi-

ately called for coffee and butter cakes, and it was decided
that the four of us would start out for Zhmerinka that very
day. But in order not to give the town of Yampol a chance
to speculate why the four of us were traveling together, it
was arranged that I would take an earlier train, and they a
later one. In the meantime, I was to find a nice inn and
order a dinner according to all the fine points of the Law.
And that was that.

I was the first to arrive in Zhmerinka. I went straight to
the best inn in town—there is only one inn in Zhmerinka
—called Odessa Inn. To start with, I made friends with the
landlady, a very kindly, hospitable Jewish woman, and I
asked her, "What have you got to eat?" Says she, "What do
you want to eat?" Say I, "Have you any fish?" Says she, "Can
be bought." Say I, "Well, and a soup?" Says she, "Soup can
be ordered, too." Say I, "Soup with what—noodles or
rice?" Says she, "Even with nuts, if you want." Say I,
"Well, and how about roast ducks, maybe?" Says she, "For
money you can get ducks, too." Say I, "Well, and something to drink?" Says she, "What do you drink?" Say I, "Is
there any beer?" Says she, "Why shouldn't there be beer?"
Say I, "Fine! And is there any wine, too?" Says she, "Anything for money." "In that event," I say, "please be good
enough, my dear woman, to prepare a dinner large
enough for eight people." Says she, "Why eight, if you are
all alone here?" Say I, "What a peculiar woman you are!
What do you care? If I say eight, eight it is! . . ."

And while we are still talking, in comes my partner—
Reb Osher, I mean—he falls upon my neck and kisses me
like a father. "I felt it in my bones," he says, "that I would
meet you here at the Odessa Inn. Can one get anything to
fortify one's soul around here?" "Why," I say, "I've just
ordered a dinner for eight." "Who is talking about din-
ners!" says he. "A dinner's a dinner, but while the two

parties are creeping toward this town, are we obliged to fast?" says he. "I see," he says to me, "that you've made yourself quite at home here, so please be good enough to have a table set for us and order a drop of brandy and some meat to drown in it. I am fainting with hunger and can hardly stand on my feet!" Thus Reb Osher—and without further delay, he goes straight to the kitchen to wash up, makes friends with the landlady, and orders everything in sight. We both sit down and have quite a spread, and while he is eating, Reb Osher tells me all about the wonders and miracles that he has achieved in Yarmelinetz: how he had to divide the Red Sea and how he had to sweat before he persuaded his nobleman to part with three thousand. . . .

"What do you mean, three thousand!" I say. "We originally agreed on nothing less than four! . . ." "Bear with me, Reb Menahem-Mendl," he says. "I know my business, or my name isn't Reb Osher! You have to realize," he says, "that my nobleman wanted to put down nothing with a zero, and all because he has such a long family tree and his wife even a longer one. He says that if he were ready to make a match with the first one that came along, they'd have to pay extra in cash. . . . In short," he says, "I had to work my head off—it was like chopping wood—and only after a good deal of sweat and labor, I managed to persuade him to give at least two thousand." "What do you mean, two thousand!" I say. "A minute ago you said three thousand!" So he says again, "Bear with me, Reb Menahem-Mendl. I am an older marriage broker than you, or my name isn't Reb Osher. Just let the two parties meet, just let the bride and groom take a look at one another—and everything will be as right as gold, God willing. Because of a miserable thousand," he says, "no match of mine has ever fallen through—or my name isn't Reb Osher, you under-

stand? However," he says, "there is one detail which keeps
me from sleeping at night." "What keeps you from sleeping, for example?" I ask. "Conscription," says he. "That's
what doesn't let me sleep. I've talked my nobleman into
believing," says he, "that your Moishe-Nissl's offspring is
still a young child—peaches and cream—but one needn't
give a hoot about conscription because Moishe-Nissl has
already wangled an exemption from military service. . . ."
"What are you babbling about, Reb Osher!" I cry.
"What conscription? Which conscription! What's all this
rubbish?" So he starts all over again, "Bear with me, Reb
Menahem-Mendl, or my name isn't Reb Osher. . . ."
"You can be called Reb Osher fifty times over," I say. "I
still don't know what you're talking about! You keep jab-
bering about conscription—what has my Moishe-Nissl got
to do with conscription? Since when are females liable to
military service?" Says Reb Osher to me, "What do you
mean, *females!* What about your Moishe-Nissl's son? . . ."
"Since when," say I, "has Moishe-Nissl a son? All he
happens to have is a daughter—a one and only daughter!"
"Am I to understand," says he, "that you also have a female? Why," he says, "haven't we been talking about a
bridegroom all this time?" "Of course, we've been talking about a bridegroom!" I say. "But I was sure it's you
on the bridegroom's side!" "And what made you think,"
says he, "that it's me on the bridegroom's side?" "And
what put it into your head," say I, "that it's *me* on the
bridegroom's side?" "So why didn't you mention it to me,"
he says, "that you have a female?" "For that matter," say
I, "did you even mention it to me that *you* have a female?
. . ." He gets annoyed and says, "You know what I'll tell
you, Menahem-Mendl? If you are a marriage broker, then
I am a rabbi!" Say I, "And if *you* are a marriage broker, then
I am a rabbi's wife!"

One word leads to another. He to me: Oaf! I to him: Liar! He to me: Good-for-nothing! I to him: Glutton! He to me: Menahem-Mendl! I to him: Drunken sot! . . . This touches him to the quick, so he up and gives me a slap. Then I get my fingers into his beard and . . . oh, what a scandal it was, God preserve and protect us! . . .

Do you understand, my dearest wife? Such a lot of expense and so much wasted time and trouble! To say nothing of the shame of it! The whole town came running to see two marriage brokers who had performed the amazing feat of matching up a pair of girls! But that cursed Osher managed immediately to disappear into thin air, leaving me to square accounts with the landlady for the dinner I had ordered for eight people. I was lucky enough to make my getaway before the two families arrived in Zhmerinka with their two brides. What happened to them, I do not know. I can only picture the disgrace. . . . But who could be a prophet and foretell that the accursed marriage broker would turn out to be a magpie, a windbag who did nothing but chatter, run around, and dash off telegrams—and with what results? Two girls betrothed to each other! . . .

Once and for all, my dearest wife, I repeat I have no luck. I may as well throw myself alive into the river! And because I am terribly depressed over this match, I must cut this short. Please God, in my next letter I'll write you everything in detail. For the time being, may the Lord grant health and success. Greet the children, God bless them—I miss them terribly—and give my kindest regards to your father and mother, to old and young, to big and small.

From me, your husband,
Menahem-Mendl.

Just remembered! The good Lord sends the balm before the blow. When I was leaving Zhmerinka, I thought the sky had fallen down upon me. If at least I had enough money for traveling expenses, I would have somehow managed to crawl home to Kasrilevka. But I figured that without sufficient money I would get stranded midway, so I might as well leave the train and stretch out across the railway tracks, Heaven forbid. But after all, it's the All-Merciful who rules this world, and so I got friendly on the train with a peculiar character, an agent-inspector who insures people against death. He started to talk me into the business, promising me a mint of money if I would become an agent. What exactly is an agent and how people can get insured against death will take too long to tell, and as this time I have overshot the mark considerably, I'll leave it for the next letter.

As above.

Book VI
TERRIBLE LUCK!
Menahem-Mendl, Agent

Menahem-Mendl from the road to his wife,
Sheineh-Sheindl, in Kasrilevka

To my dear, wise, and modest helpmeet, Sheineh-Sheindl,
long may she live!

Firstly, I am come to inform you that I am, by the
grace of God, well and in good cheer. May the Lord, blessed
be His name, grant that we always hear from one another
none but the best, the most comforting, and the happiest
of tidings—amen.

And Secondly, I want you to know, my dearest
wife, that I am now a refugee. That is to say, I have had to
bolt. I managed to escape misfortune by the skin of my
teeth—very terrible misfortune! I thank the Almighty
for having delivered me from peril. I found myself in such
a pretty kettle of fish, God alone knows how I managed
to squirm out of it. All I can say is that I was close to being
clapped into jail and maybe even sent to Siberia for hard
labor, although I am as innocent as you in the whole affair. As your mother says, "When you have terrible luck,
it follows you from door to door and through the gate.
. . ." But now that the Almighty has come to my aid and I
have managed to escape disaster in time, I am sitting down
to write you everything in detail, from beginning to end.

From my last letter you will perhaps recall in what a fix
I was after that pretty betrothal of two females, may we all

be spared the same. At that time I figured it was the end to everything. Menahem-Mendl was finished. However, what happened was that I met a character, an agent, an inspector in the Aquitable, who insures people against death and makes money on it hand over fist. This agent pulled out a notebook and showed me how many people he had already insured against death and how many people have already died on him. In this kind of business, the more people die, the better—for both the dead and the living. You will probably ask why. Well, the reason is really very simple. For instance, Aquitable insures me against death for ten thousand shekels. All I have to do is pay a mere two or three hundred a year until I die. Then there are two alternatives: If I pass away, God forbid, during the first year, it's *your* good fortune since you are my wife, and ten thousand shekels is quite a pretty sum. But what happens if I go on living? Then it is Aquitable's good fortune.

Lots of people are working for Aquitable as agents— most of them Jews who have wives and children and who also have to make both ends meet on God's earth. So am I any worse than they? The trouble is, not everyone can become an agent. An agent must, first and foremost, be well dressed—and I mean *well:* a fine suit of clothes, collar and cuffs (they can be made of cardboard, but they have to be white), a handsome tie—and it goes without saying that he must wear a hat. But the most important thing is— language, the gift of speech. An agent has to know the language. That is to say, he has to know how to talk! Talk against time; talk at random; talk glibly; talk himself out of breath; talk you into things; talk in circles—in short, he has to talk and talk and talk until you surrender and get yourself insured against death. And that's all there is to it! In short, that character—the agent-inspector—saw at a glance that I would make a good agent, a first-class inquisitor.

Now, my dearest wife, I must explain to you the difference between an agent-inspector and an agent-inquisitor. An agent-inquisitor is an ordinary agent who insures people against death, whereas an agent-inspector is a senior agent who appoints ordinary agents. Then there are also district agent-inspectors whose business is to appoint agent-inspectors, and over and above all those agents, inquisitors, inspectors, and district heads, there is an overlord who rules over them all and who is called an inspector general. There is nobody higher than he in the whole wide world. Naturally, in order to become a general, you must first start as an inquisitor; then you become an inspector, then a district inspector, and so on. And if, by the grace of God, you've served a long time and worked hard enough till you've become a general—then you are on Easy Street for the rest of your life. There are, says my character, some generals who spend no less than thirty thousand a year!

To make a long story short, he started talking me into becoming an agent. So I thought it over carefully. What, in fact, have I got to lose? Just figure it out: If I succeed—well and good. If not—I'll be back where I started from! He says I don't have to invest my legacy in the business. On the contrary, I'll even get an advance, he says—that is, they'll give me a few shekels on account in order to cover my expenses, get decently dressed, and buy a portfolio. Considering all this, you must admit it was quite a good proposition. So I let myself be talked into it, and in a lucky moment I became an agent.

But it's more easily said than done. Because, first of all, an agent has to meet the general. If the general doesn't give his signature—that puts the lid on! So the inspector took me to Odessa—at his own expense, too!—in order to present me to his general at the Aquitable, who lords it over more than twenty districts and, they say, has under his thumb almost eighteen hundred agents.

It's no use even trying to describe to you the greatness of that general. That is to say, he himself is not as great as the racket that's raised around him. He has large sharp eyes, a bright little face and little red cheeks, and his name is Yevzerell. The general's office occupies an entire building with hundreds of rooms. There are a lot of desks, benches, books, and papers, and agents mill about, rushing and pushing, coming and going, talking and shouting; telegrams are flying back and forth—it's bedlam!

Before anybody manages to make his way into the general's office, he has to pass all the seven circles of purgatory. By the time I was brought before this Yevzerell, I was halfdead. However, he received me very nicely, even offered me a seat, treated me to a cigarette, and asked me who I was, what I was, and what my business was. So I told him everything from beginning to end: how I was on my way to Kishinev and blundered into Odessa by mistake; how I dealt in London there; how from Odessa I went to Yehupetz, where I roved about the exchange, buying and selling Putilovs, Lilliputs, and other papers to the tune of millions; and then how I became (may you be spared the same) a broker in sugar and gold, in houses and estates, in forests and factories; and afterward how I even became a writer, and still later a matchmaker—how I simmered and seethed and bubbled and foamed and made a great big noise all over the world, and how in the end, it all turned out to be a case of bad luck following me from door to door and through the gate. . . .

After he listened to the whole story, the general rose, put his hand on my shoulder, and said, "You know what I have to say to you, Mr. Menahem-Mendl? I like you! You have a good name, and, thank God, you know how to talk. I foresee that you'll be a big agent in due course—a really great one! For the time being, you'll get an advance. You'll go out into the world; you'll travel through Jewish cities and towns where you are well known—and may luck follow you! . . ." And that was that.

As soon as I received several shekels from them, I got myself dressed up like a prince. If you were to see me in my new clothes, you wouldn't recognize me. I also bought myself a portfolio—a big one—which they packed for me with a wagonload of notebooks and papers. And I started to travel over the face of God's earth.

My first goal was Bessarabia the blessed, the land of milk and honey. There, I was told, it's easy to do wonderful business—no end of insurance. But as luck would have it, I had to commemorate the day of my father's death, so between trains I found myself in a little town, far from nowhere. What I did not know was that this town was famous throughout the world for its rascals, rogues, swindlers, perjurers, and informers. Oh, why didn't it burn to an ash before I ever set foot in it! But since misfortune was in the books—I had to commemorate my father's death in this cursed town and sink in the bog, may the Lord preserve us! In fact, something told me I wouldn't leave this place the same man. But if one has to arrange a memorial for the dead, is there any choice?

So I went straight to the synagogue and arrived just in time for the evening prayers. When the prayers were over, the beadle comes up to me and says, "Memorial?" Say I, "Memorial." Says he to me, "Where does a Jew come from?" Say I, "Out of the wide world." Says he, "What may your name be?" Say I, "Menahem-Mendl." "Well, allow me to greet you!" and he stretches out his hand. All the other worshipers follow suit, and before long I am encircled by a group of men, all trying to pump me: Who am I; where do I come from; what is my business? . . . I tell them I'm an agent. So they ask, "An agent of what—machinery?" I say, "As a matter of fact, no. I am an agent-inquisitor for Aquitable." So they ask, "What kind of plague is that?" I tell them that I insure people against death. And I try to explain to them exactly how it is possible to insure people against death. They stare at me, their jaws hanging loose, as if I had told them there's a cow jumping over the moon. However, I noticed a couple of chaps among the crowd, one of them tall, thin, and crooked, with a very shiny nose, which was also crooked, and with a habit of picking hairs out of his beard as he talked. The other one was short, broad in the beam, dark as a gypsy, with a single eye that looked northward and had a sly twinkle in it. Even when he talked seriously, you had the impression that he was smiling. These two apparently did understand what it meant to insure people against death, because I caught them exchanging peculiar glances and overheard one mutter to the other, "This ought to go well. . . ." I immediately gathered that they were quite different from the rest; obviously they understood business, and with them one could make a deal. And that was that.

No sooner do I emerge from the synagogue than these two follow me, catch up with me, and say, "Where are you rushing, Reb Menahem-Mendl? Wait a minute, we want to ask you something: Do you intend to do business in this town, in this hole?" Say I, "Why not?" Says the tall man, the one with the crooked nose, "With our brethren, the children of Israel? . . ." and his one-eyed friend chimes in, "The only thing you can do with Jews is to share a noodle pudding." Say I, "So what would you advise me to do?" Says the tall one, "To deal only with gentile noble-men." "Long live nobility!" chimes in the one-eyed fel-low. . . .

Talking in this vein, we stroll along, and we talk and talk until we talk ourselves into a deal. It appears these two fellows have a nobleman all their own—a big, rich Bes-sarabian, thanks to whom they often manage to turn a penny. In their opinion, he could be insured very prop-erly. . . . Say I, "And why not? It would be an honor! On the contrary," say I, "let's get going and make this deal in partnership. I'm in no hurry to get rich. . . ." So it was decided that tomorrow, please God, in the synagogue, during the first morning prayer, they would bring me their nobleman's reply. There was, however, one important point: They asked me to keep the matter strictly secret; that is to say, I was not to drop even a hint at my inn that I had met them and talked business with them.

At daybreak, I hurried to the synagogue to join the very first morning service. The prayers done with, I looked around—my chaps were not in sight. I waited till the sec-ond service was over—there was still no sign of them. Why didn't I ask for their names and addresses, fool that I was! Should I ask the beadle? But I was afraid—I promised them to keep it secret. . . . After I had given up all hope, they finally appeared with their prayer shawls and phylac-teries. When I saw them, my heart leaped for joy. I had to restrain myself from going up to them and asking what news they had for me—that wouldn't have been good manners. They made short work of the prayers, packed up their prayer shawls and phylacteries, and dashed out—and I at their heels. "Well?" I say to them. "Mum's the word!" they tell me. "Don't talk in the street—you don't know what our town is like, may it burn to an ash for your sake! Just walk behind us, and follow us home. There we can talk

business and at the same time get a bite to eat. . . ." So
says Crooked Nose; he winks to One-Eye, and One-Eye
immediately vanishes. The two of us walk through dark,
dank, narrow lanes—he leading and I following. We walk
and walk until, by the grace of God, we finally arrive at his
home safe and sound.

We entered a small, dark, smoke-blackened room with
a lot of flies all over the walls and ceiling, a hand-painted
Biblical picture hanging on the east wall, a red cover on
the table and a lampshade decorated with faded paper
flowers. Sitting near the oven we found a tiny, dirty woman
with a pale, frightened face. The little woman gave her
husband a frightened glance. As he passed her, he barked,
"Food!" In an instant, there appeared a white tablecloth,
a loaf of white bread, a bottle of brandy, and some tidbits.
Before long, the door opened, and One-Eye entered the
room; after him in rolled a creature weighing about three
hundred pounds, with a huge, blue nose, fat, hairy hands,
and a pair of peculiar legs—thick in the thigh but so thin at
the ankle that it was hard to believe they could support
such an enormously heavy carcass.

This creature was the Bessarabian nobleman. The moment he caught sight of the bottle of brandy on the table,
out of his great fat belly there issued a great fat voice,
speaking in dialect: *"Otzeh dobreh dilo!"* (Just the job!)
After each one of us took a drop of spirits (the nobleman
took two drops), both my fellows started to talk to him
about corn and wheat. In the meantime, One-Eye whis-
pered to me, "This baron is ready to burst—he must have
about a thousand measures of wheat, to say nothing of
oats. . . . Don't take any notice of the rags he's wearing
—he is simply stingy. . . ." The tall one continued talking
to the baron; he advised him not to sell his flour because
wheat was going up in price; he would do better to hold

on to it till winter. "*Otzeh dobreh dilo!*" the baron re-
peated over and over again. He drained glass after glass
and shoveled in the food, like a man who had just ended a
fast, blowing out his lips and snorting through his nose.

After the meal was over, the tall one said to me, "Now
you can talk to the baron about your business." So I re-
tired to a corner of the room with the baron and began
preaching a sermon to him, I myself don't know how it
came to me! I gave him to understand how important it is
for certain people to be insured even if they are as rich as
Croesus. "As a matter of fact, the richer you are," say I,
"the more important it is to get insured, because for a rich
man to lose money in his old age is a thousand times worse
than for a pauper. A pauper," I say, "is used to misery, but
when a rich man is left penniless, God forbid, it is worse
than being dead. *Yak napissano oo nass,* I say"—that's
what's written in our books—"*Oni hashuv kamett*—a
pauper is about as important as a corpse. That is to say, it's
worse to be poor than to be dead. Therefore, your honor,"
I say, "you ought to get yourself insured against the day
of your death in a hundred and twenty years," I say, "for
ten thousand." "*Otzeh dobreh dilo!*" says the baron, blowing out his lips like bellows. I feel the gift of speech bub-
bling inside of me, my lips breathe fire, and I want to continue talking, but the tall one interrupts, "Turn off the tap!
Take the policy, and fill it out. . . ." One-Eye brings me a
pen and a bottle of ink, I fill out whatever is necessary, and
when the time comes for him to sign, the poor baron starts
sweating profusely until he manages to set down his signature. Then I go with him to a doctor who examines him; I
receive a deposit, give him a receipt—and the deal is done.

In the evening, on my return to the inn, I order supper,
very happy and pleased with myself. The innkeeper says to
me, "What's new with you?" "What can be new?" say I.

"May one congratulate you?" "Congratulate on what?" I ask. "On that little deal you've just finished. . . ." "What little deal?" say I, pretending innocence. "With the baron," he says. "Which baron?" "The fat one." "How do you know I've made a deal with a baron?" I ask. "If he's a baron," says he, "I am a rabbi's wife." "So what is he?" "He's a horned snake," says the innkeeper and bursts out laughing right in my face.

I sit down next to him and begin to plead with him to tell me what he means by a horned snake, and how he knows where I've been and what I've been doing. In short, the innkeeper apparently realized from my questions that I was as innocent as a newborn lamb, because he took pity on me, locked himself up with me in a separate room, and started telling me stories about my two partners that made my hair rise on end. It seems those two fellows are nothing but ordinary swindlers and rascals, he says, second to none in the whole wide world. "Already," he says, "they've managed to pull off such criminal feats in their lifetime that if ever they are caught, they'll be dragged far, far away. . . . But it is their unholy luck," says he, "that they always manage to find a third partner for a scapegoat, while they themselves get away with murder. . . . As for the baron," he says, "whom they introduced to you as a very rich Bessarabian, he is nothing but an ordinary tramp and an illustrious sot . . ." he says. "And it isn't the baron whom you've insured against death—it is somebody else who is either on his deathbed or has already mingled his bones with the dust. . . . Do you understand," says he, "what this smells of?"

When I heard this, I was struck all in a heap. All I needed now, to add to my many achievements, was to be clapped into jail. So I wasted no time on long speeches, immediately sprinted to the railway station, and ran wherever my feet

would carry me. I didn't even want to see my two late partners again—they could go to the blazes together with their
baron, together with their town and all of Bessarabia, together with all this business of insuring people against
death which can lead you to such a calamity. . . . May
the good Lord send me a better kind of business if I only
reach some refuge in safety. And because I am now in the
midst of a very long journey, I must cut this short. Please
God, in my next letter I'll write you everything in detail
from Hamburg. For the time being, may the Lord send
health and success. Greet the children, God bless them.
God grant I find them well and strong, in happiness, in
joy and in good fortune. Give my kindest regards to your
father and mother, to old and young, to big and small.

From me, your husband,
Menahem-Mendl.

Just remembered! I forgot to tell you where I
am going. My dearest wife, I am going to America! I am
not alone. I am traveling with a whole group. That is to say,
for the time being, we are going only to Hamburg. But
from Hamburg we shall sail for America. Why America all
of a sudden? Because they say that in America life is good
for Jews. They say that gold is rolling in the streets, yours
for the picking. Their money is reckoned in dollars, and
people—people are held above rubies! As for Jews—they
are considered the cream of the lot in America! Everybody
assures me that in America I'll make good, please God—
and they mean, *good.* Everyone is going to America these
days because there is nothing to do here. Absolutely nothing. All business is finished. Well, if everybody is going,
why shouldn't I go, too? What have I got to lose? . . .
Only you are not to worry, my dearest wife, and for mercy's
sake, don't think ill of me. Believe me, I shall not forget

you, perish the thought—neither you nor our dear little
children, God bless them. I'll work day and night, nothing
will be too difficult for me, and when I am successful, please
God—and that I *will* be successful is as sure as the sun
shines—I'll send steamship tickets for you and the children,
and I'll bring you to America, and you'll live with me in
comfort and in honor like a princess, wanting for nothing
and having everything your heart desires, and I'll watch
over you, I won't let a speck of dust fall upon you, because
it is about time—so help me God!—that you too should
have some joy of life! Only please do not worry and do not
take it to heart—for our God is the All-Wise, the All-
Merciful, and the All-Powerful!

As above.